"I want a puppy,"

Nina said to the woman at Riverbend Animal Control. "Something perky."

The woman nodded, and Nina followed her through a door, determined to pick herself out the perkiest birthday present on four paws. She'd always wanted a dog, but her ex-husband hadn't understood. "Dogs shed," he'd said when she'd suggested they get one as a wedding present to each other. She should have known that was A Sign. But no, she'd married him anyway.

Nina peered into a cage. The pups were darling. Climbing over one another and tumbling and barking. Perky.

She glanced in the other cage almost by accident. Then she froze.

There was only one dog in the cage. He was midsize and depressed, too big for her apartment and too melancholy for her state of mind. Nina tried to turn back to the puppies, but somehow, she couldn't.

Nina did not need this dog. He bowed his head a little as if it had grown too heavy for him, and his ears sagged. She took a step back, and he sighed and lay down, not expecting anything at all.

Any dog but this one.

She turned to the attendant and said, "I'll take him."

Dear Reader,

Welcome to another month of LOVE & LAUGHTER, a look at the lighter side of love. Taking our inspiration from the beloved screwball comedies of yesterday to the romantic comedies of today, we searched high and low, far and wide, just about everywhere, in fact, for authors who love and write romance and comedy. The results, if we dare be so immodest, have been absolutely fabulous.

This month *New York Times* bestselling author Kasey Michaels, known both for her romance fiction from Silhouette and mainstream historical romance novels, delights with *Five's a Crowd*. Her comic tale of lovers who never get to be alone is warm and emotional and funny. We are thrilled to have Kasey in the LOVE & LAUGHTER lineup.

RITA Award-winning Jennifer Crusie simply continues to amaze us with her talent. She has very quickly become a reader favorite, and *Anyone But You* will win her many more fans. Her heroine, Nina, was beginning her life fresh—new job, new apartment. No husband. All she wanted was a puppy. A happy, perky puppy. Instead she got Fred. Part basset, part beagle, part manic-depressive...and things only get crazier from there.

With love—and laughter,

Malle Vallik

Malle Vallik
Associate Senior Editor

ANYONE BUT YOU
Jennifer Crusie

Harlequin Books

TORONTO • NEW YORK • LONDON
AMSTERDAM • PARIS • SYDNEY • HAMBURG
STOCKHOLM • ATHENS • TOKYO • MILAN
MADRID • WARSAW • BUDAPEST • AUCKLAND

ISBN 0-373-44004-9

ANYONE BUT YOU

Copyright © 1996 by Jennifer Crusie

Jennifer Crusie began writing romances as part of her research for her doctoral dissertation. A win in the Harlequin Short Reads Contest led to her first sale in 1992, a Stolen Moments novella called *Sizzle*. She has since published five Harlequin Temptations, *Manhunting*, *Getting Rid of Bradley* (for which she won the 1995 RWA Rita Award for Best Short Contemporary), *Strange Bedpersons*, *What the Lady Wants* and *Charlie All Night*. She lives in southern Ohio where she is currently finishing her M.F.A. and Ph.D. and working on her first single title novel. She is very pleased and proud to be part of the new Love & Laughter line.

For Meg Ruley,
Fred's godmother and
my partner in crime and lit-ra-chure

Acknowledgment

My heartfelt thanks to Laurie Grant
for her ER expertise

1

THE LAST THING Nina Askew needed was Fred.

"I want a puppy," she said to the dumpy brown-uniformed woman behind the scarred metal counter at Riverbend Animal Control. "Something perky."

"Perky." The woman sighed. "Sure. We got perky." She jerked her head toward the gray metal door at the end of the counter. "Through there, one step down."

"Right." Nina shoved her short dark curls behind her ears, grabbed her purse and walked through the door, determined to pick herself out the perkiest birthday present on four paws. So what if yesterday had been her fortieth birthday? Forty was a good age for a woman. It meant freedom. Especially freedom from her overambitious ex-husband and their overpriced suburban castle which had finally sold after a year of open-house hell. There was something good: she was out of that damn house.

And now she was forty. Well, she was delighted to be forty. After all, that was the reason she was getting a dog of her own.

The attendant joined her and said, "This way," and Nina followed her toward yet another heavy metal door. She was going to get a puppy. She'd always wanted a dog, but Guy hadn't understood. "Dogs shed," he'd said when she'd suggested they get one as a wedding present to each other. She should have known that was A Sign. But no, she'd

married him anyway and moved into that designer mausoleum of a house. And then she'd spent fifteen years following her husband's career around, without a dog, in a house she'd grown to hate. Sixteen years in the house, if she counted this last year in divorced-woman limbo, waiting for it to sell. But now she had freedom and an apartment of her own and a great, if precarious, job. The only thing she needed was a warm, cheerful body to come home to.

The attendant opened the door, and the faint barking Nina had heard before became frantic and shrill. Nina stepped into the concrete cell block and stopped, blown out of her self-absorption by the row of gray metal cages where dogs barked to get her attention. She let her breath out, horrified. "Oh, God, this is awful."

"Spay your pets." The attendant stopped in front of the next to last cage. "Here you go." She jerked her head again. "Perky."

Nina went to join the woman and peered into the cage the attendant had shown her. The pups were darling—some sort of tiny, bright-eyed, spotted mixed breed—climbing over one another and tumbling and whining and barking. Perky as hell. Now all she had to do was choose one...

She moved closer and glanced in the last cage almost by accident. Then she froze.

There was only one dog in the cage, and it was midsize and depressed, too big for her apartment and too melancholy for her state of mind. Nina tried to turn back to the puppies, but somehow, she couldn't. The dog had huge bags under his dark eyes, and hunched shoulders, and a white coat blotched with what looked like giant liver spots. He sat on the damp concrete like a bulked-up vulture and stared at her, not barking, not moving. He looked like her great-uncle Fred had before he'd died when she was six.

She'd liked her uncle Fred, and then one day his heart had gone, as her mother had put it, and that had been it.

"Hello," she said, and the dog lifted his head a little, so she stooped down and reached through the cage doors to scratch him behind the ears. He looked at her and then closed his eyes in appreciation for the scratch.

"What's wrong with him?" Nina asked the attendant.

"Nothing," the attendant said. "He's part basset, part beagle." She checked the card on his cage. "Or he might be psychic. This is his last day."

Nina's eyes opened wide. "You mean . . ."

"Yep." The attendant sliced her hand across her throat.

Nina looked back at the dog. The dog looked back at Nina, death in his eyes.

Oh, God.

She stood and shoved her hair behind her ears, trying to look efficient and practical in an effort to be efficient and practical. She did not need this dog. She needed a happy, perky puppy, and on his best day, this dog would look like a professional mourner. And he wasn't even a puppy.

Any dog but this one.

She looked down at the dog one last time, and her hair fell forward, a curly black frame for his depression. He bowed his head a little as if it had grown too heavy for him, and his ears sagged with the bow.

She could not take this dog. He was too depressed. He was too big. He was too old. She took a step back, and he sighed and lay down, not expecting anything at all, resigned to the cold hard floor and no one to love him and the certainty of death in the morning.

At least, that was what Nina was sure he was resigned to. She couldn't stand it. She turned to the attendant, and said, "I'll take him."

The attendant raised an eyebrow. "That's your idea of perky?"

Nina gestured to the puppies. "They'll all be adopted, right?"

"Sure."

Nina took one long last glance at the tumbling, chubby puppies. Prozac with four legs and a tail. Then she looked at the other dog, depressed, alone, too old to be cute anymore if he ever had been. "I have a lot in common with this dog," she told the attendant. "And besides, I'd never sleep again knowing I could have saved him and didn't."

The attendant shook her head. "You can't save them all."

"Well, I can save this one." Nina crouched to the dog's level. "It's okay, Fred. I just rescued your butt."

The dog rolled his eyes up to stare at her.

"No, don't thank me. Glad to do it for you." Nina stood up and followed the attendant down the hall. At the end, she turned, and Fred moved forward, pressing his nose through the bars. "Hey, it's okay," Nina called to him. "I'm coming right back as soon as I get you sprung from this joint."

Fred moaned and stumbled back into the depths of the cage.

"Oh, yeah, *you're* going to cheer me up," Nina said and went to sign the papers and pay the fee.

He didn't get much happier when the attendant opened the cage and he waddled out into Nina's arms, fragrant beyond belief. "You stink, Fred," she told him, and then she picked him up and held him to her, telling herself that her silk suit was dry-cleanable, and that at least it was brown and so was most of Fred so the dog hair wouldn't show. He looked up at her and she added, "And you weigh a ton." He was like dead weight in her arms, round and bulky, and

most of his weight seemed to be centered in his rear end, which gave him a definite droop as she balanced his hip on hers. Still, as much as he reeked, it felt good to have her arms wrapped around him. "I saved you, Fred," she whispered into his ear, and he twitched as her breath tickled him, patient but not by any means enthused about the new turn of events.

He perked up a little when she carried him out into the May sunlight, but he seemed annoyed when she tried to balance all of his weight on one hip while she maneuvered open the door to her white Civic.

"I was planning...on getting...a puppy," she told him, breathing hard as she used her other hip to push the car door farther open. "I wasn't planning...on getting a... part basset...part beagle...part *lead-ass*." She managed to heave him into the seat and close the door, and then she leaned against the car to get her breath back. Fred rocked back and forth as he situated himself on the blue upholstery, and then he turned and smeared his nose on the window. "Good." Nina sighed. "Make yourself at home."

She got in the Civic and stuck the key in the ignition. Fred put his paws on the window ledge and smeared his nose higher. Nina thought longingly of the puppies. "You're making me ill." She leaned across him and began to roll down the window halfway. "Don't jump out. Things just got better for you."

Fred turned at the sound of her voice, and as she stretched over him still cranking the window, he looked deep into her eyes. Nina stopped rolling and stared back into the warm brown depths. He really was a sweet dog. Of course he wasn't being peppy. In his situation, she'd be cautious, too. He didn't know anything about her. She didn't know anything about where he'd been. Maybe his previous owner had been mean to him. It didn't matter.

What mattered was that he needed love. Everybody needed love. Even she needed love. And now she had Fred.

Fred.

Nina closed her eyes. Terrific. She had Fred. Even her best friend was going to think she was nuts. "You bought a *what?*" Charity was going to say, and then when she saw Fred, middle-aged, broken-down and tired, she was going to—Nina looked into Fred's patient brown eyes again and felt ashamed. "It's okay, Fred." She stroked the top of his head. "You're my dog now. It's okay."

Fred met her eyes, made his decision, squared his shoulders and lunged at her, licking her from chin to forehead with one sweeping slurp.

"Oh, *Fred.*" Nina burst into tears and wrapped her arms around him. His body was fat and warm and wriggly, and Nina hugged him tighter, so glad to have someone alive in her life again and so relieved to finally be able to cry out the frustration and loneliness that she didn't even care the someone had four legs and smelled like rank canine. "We're going to be so happy together, Fred," she told him, sobbing. "We really are. We're going to be wonderful together."

Fred sighed and began to lick the tears from her face, which made Nina cry even harder. It was the best she'd felt in weeks.

She gave one final sniff and let go of Fred to put the car in gear so she could show him his new home and call his aunt Charity to come meet him.

"You have family now, Fred," she told him. "You're going home."

ALEX MOORE WAS stretched out on a bed in an empty examining room in the Riverbend General ER, trying to forget his family and get some sleep before another emergency

erupted, when his older brother came in and dropped a brown paper bag with a six-pack of beer in it on his stomach.

"Hey!" Alex curled to absorb the blow and then saw it was Max and stretched back out again. Pain in conjunction with his family was nothing new. "I'm sleeping. Go away. And take that damn beer with you before somebody sees it."

Max pulled the beer out of the sack and peeled off a can. He popped the tab and left the five remaining beers on Alex's stomach as he collapsed into an orange plastic chair. The chair scraped and screeched on the floor, and Max's purple silk shirt clashed against the green wall. Alex winced and closed his eyes, hoping Max would take the hint and leave.

Max didn't. "You know, if you didn't spend your nights chasing women, you wouldn't get this tired during your shifts," he said and sipped his beer.

Alex didn't bother to open his eyes. "I did not spend my night chasing a woman. I took Debbie to dinner. She started talking about kids. I took her home. Story of my love life."

"It's because you've got that blond good-guy look," Max told him. "You've got nice guy written all over you. Now me, I look like a rat."

Alex kept his eyes closed as a hint. "Yeah, you do. Go away, rat."

"Of course, it's too late to pretend you're a rat around here since everybody knows you. You should have just changed the subject. 'Speaking of kids, Debbie, how about some sex?' You've got to learn to be faster on your feet."

Alex thought about snarling at him to go away and decided against it. He liked Max a lot, and given his family, a relative he was usually happy to see was a rarity. "I don't

want to be faster on my feet. I just want to spend some nice quiet evenings with a woman who wants me more than she wants kids or a wedding ring. All the women I know have biological clocks and a burning need to commit. I want a woman who has a burning need to be with me and watch old movies and laugh. But right now, all I want is to sleep, which is why you're leaving."

Max swallowed some more beer. "It's because you're a doctor. Women always want to marry doctors."

Alex opened one eye, trying to ignore the purple shirt against the green wall. "You're a doctor. How come it doesn't happen to you?"

"I try not to date anybody more than twice," Max said. "It keeps the subject from coming up."

"That's real mature of you, Max." Alex closed his eye again. "Now go away. For once there are no disasters out there, and I need some sleep."

Max sipped his beer again. "This is your last day as a twenty-something, kid. How does it feel to be old?"

"You tell me," Alex said. "You're the one pushing forty."

"Thirty-six is not forty," Max said with dignity. "And you're going to lose your hair before I do. It's already creeping back from your forehead. I can see it from here. It's because you're blond. Dark-haired guys like me never lose it." He tipped the beer into his mouth this time and sucked up the last half of the can.

"Tell me you're not still doing rounds."

"Finished an hour ago." Max pitched the can into a nearby wastebasket and slumped, as much as he could, in the plastic chair. "You off soon?"

"Three more hours. Go away."

"So you ready for tomorrow?"

"It's my birthday," Alex said with his eyes shut. "It's not something I have to get ready for. Other people have to get ready for it. You, for example. Go buy me something expensive. You make the big bucks."

"Exactly," Max said. "And you know why."

Alex groaned and rolled away from his brother, who lunged to get the five-pack of beer as it tipped toward the floor.

"Hey!" Max said. "Avoid reality if you have to, but don't spill the beer."

Alex kept his back to him. "I'm not avoiding reality. I'm avoiding you. Go away."

"I am reality, buddy," Max said, and Alex heard the scrape of the plastic chair as his brother sat down again and the clank as he put the cans on the floor. "I ran into Dad just now. He was looking for you."

Alex groaned again.

Max's voice was sympathetic. "Yeah, I know. He wants to have dinner with you tomorrow."

"No," Alex said.

"I told him you would. Hell, it's not like you could get out of it. He said to meet him at The Levee at seven. For drinks first."

"Oh, hell." Alex rolled onto his back again and stared at the stained acoustic ceiling. "You could have told him I was sick. You could have told him that you'd diagnosed me with something ugly and catching."

"I'm a gynecologist," Max said. "What was I supposed to tell him? You got a yeast infection so you can't do dinner?"

"Would he have noticed?"

"Yeah," Max said. "He was working, so he was sober."

"Great. Just what I wanted on my birthday, to pour the old man into a cab at midnight."

"I took care of that," Max said. "I told him we had plans at nine. He understood."

Alex gave him a withering look. "So I get to pour him into a cab at nine. Thank you."

"It gets worse." Max beamed at him, cheerful as always. "He said your mother's coming to town tomorrow."

Alex sat up. "My mother's flying in for my birthday?"

"No," Max said. "She's flying in for a one-day seminar on the new laser technology. It just worked out that it's your birthday."

"Thank God." Alex flopped back down on the pillow. "For one awful minute, I thought she was going maternal on me."

"She told Dad she wants to have lunch with you," Max said. "Noon at the Hilton. Be on time, she's speaking at one." He picked up another beer from the floor and cracked it. "It's a shame you're still on duty. You could have one of these."

"My mother," Alex said to the ceiling. "An hour with my mother."

"You've got an hour with my mother, too," Max said after he'd taken another swig. "She wants to have a drink with you at four. She has surgery at one, so she figures she'll be free by then."

"I can stand an hour with your mother," Alex said. "I think."

"And I imagine Stella will be calling," Max began.

"She already did." Alex rubbed his hand over his eyes. "Breakfast tomorrow before she makes her rounds."

Max winced. "Do you suppose she does everything in the morning because she's the oldest?"

"No, she does everything in the morning because she's a pain in the ass," Alex said. "Even if she is my favorite relative."

"Hey!" Max straightened in his chair. "What about me? I kept you from having to spend the entire evening justifying your lack of career to the old man. You owe me."

"I have a career," Alex said for the millionth time. "I'm a doctor."

"Yeah, but you picked the wrong specialty," Max said. "You have to pick upscale, not ER. They made me, now they're going to make you. Cardiologist, oncologist, gynecologist—"

"No," Alex said. "I like what I'm doing. Go away. I'm trying to sleep."

A dark-haired little nurse poked her head in the door. "Hey, Alex, we need you. Accident coming in. Let's go." She disappeared again before he sat up.

Alex swung his feet around to the side of the bed and glared at Max. "If it hadn't been for you, I could have had a whole fifteen minutes of unconsciousness."

"That's another thing," Max said. "If you weren't an ER specialist, she'd have called you Dr. Moore."

The nurse poked her head back in. "Alex, let's *go*. Oh, hi, Max. Didn't see you there." She frowned at him. "Get rid of that beer *now*."

"Hi, Zandy." Max lifted his beer to her. "You're looking good."

She was gone before he finished his sentence.

"The respect she has for you is awesome," Alex said. "Must be because you're not an ER specialist."

"I dated her once," Max said.

"That explains it." Alex stood up and headed for the door. "Go away. I have to work."

"Don't forget tomorrow," Max called after him. "Family day. The whole Farkle family."

"Right," Alex muttered under his breath as he strode down the green-tiled hall. "Dr. Farkle, and Dr. Farkle, and Dr. Farkle, and Dr. Farkle, and Dr. Farkle."

"What?" Zandy asked him as she tried to catch up with him.

"Don't ever go into the family business, Zan," Alex said. "It's hell being low man on the dynasty."

"They trying to talk you out of the ER?" Zandy skipped a couple of times to keep up with him, her legs a good six inches shorter than his, so he slowed for her.

"Yep," Alex said.

"Don't do it."

Alex looked down at her, surprised. "No?"

"No," Zandy said. "You need this place. And it needs you. Ignore them. They're all suits."

Alex grinned at her. "Even Max?"

"Max is an ape," Zandy said. "But you're the good guy. Stay with us."

"Well, I'm planning on it," Alex began and then he heard the sirens and moved toward the doors, forgetting Zandy and Max and the whole Farkle family as he went to do what he loved best, saving lives on the run.

"YOU GOT a *what*?" Charity stood in the middle of Nina's high-ceilinged apartment and stared at Fred, amazed.

"Charity, this is not just any dog." Nina tensed, still doubtful herself about the wisdom of buying an animal for comfort. Charity wouldn't buy a dog for comfort. She'd buy a red leather miniskirt at the boutique she managed, yank her long kinky red hair up on top of her head and tie it in a knot with a black stocking, and go out and find a new man. At least, that's what she'd done the last time one

of her relationships had pancaked on her, before she'd found Sean, her One True Love. Sean was actually her Twelfth True Love, but as Charity said, who was counting?

Since Nina's chances of wearing a leather miniskirt were slim to none, she sighed and turned her attention back to Fred, sitting like a lump in the middle of her hardwood floor, looking up at her with bemused adoration. Fred was better than a leather miniskirt. He might not get her a new man, but he'd give her unconditional love. Fred was definitely better.

Charity didn't see it that way. "You move out of that mansion on Lehigh Terrace and into this apartment in this Victorian hovel, on the *third floor* of this Victorian hovel, and there's not even an elevator—"

"If you wouldn't wear four-inch heels, two flights of stairs would not be a problem," Nina murmured.

"—but that's not bad enough, you've got to *get* a dog." Charity blinked down at Fred. "That is a dog, isn't it?"

Fred stood up, turned his back on her and walked away across the floor, his butt swaying majestically.

"Charity, I need Fred," Nina said. "I feel better already. He has personality."

Charity nodded. "That's what I smell. His personality."

"I didn't want to give him a bath right away." Nina watched Fred as he explored the living room, stopping to investigate her fig tree. "Don't even think about it, Fred," she warned him. Then she said to Charity, "I wanted him to feel at home first. He's only been here an hour, but I had to call you right away. I knew you'd want to meet him."

"If he's been here an hour, he's seen home." Charity surveyed the apartment with disgust. "How you could move from your place to this..."

"I didn't move from my place, I moved from Guy's place." Nina followed Charity's eyes around the room, caressing the oak wainscoting and the tiny beige print wallpaper, the veneer fireplace and the fat ruby-upholstered couch and lopsided chair. "This is my place, the first place I've ever had that's all mine. I loved it the first time I saw it. I've been here a month now, and I feel more at home than I did after sixteen years in that mausoleum of Guy's." The thought of Guy made her shake her head. "We should never have gotten married. We didn't want any of the same things. I never wanted that house on Lehigh Terrace. He never wanted a dog." Fred began to move again, and Nina felt the tension ease out of her shoulders as she watched the miscellaneous collection of independent canine parts that was Fred move past her on his way to the couch. "I always wanted a dog. And now I have Fred."

Fred sniffed the couch again. He'd sniffed it several times since he'd arrived, but now he made a decision. His haunches quivered and tensed as he crouched, and then with a mighty leap he flung himself onto the overstuffed cushions, hanging there for a long moment, a triumph of hope over biology, only to slide slowly back to the floor and land with a soft thud as his butt failed to achieve lift-off.

He took it pretty well, considering.

Charity looked at her as if she were demented. "And you're going to run up and down the stairs twenty-six times a night to water this animal, right? And what about during the day? You work, for God's sake. I can just see Jessica's face if you bring Fred into the office." She shook her head, and her red ringlets bounced as they swung back and forth. "You're nuts. I love you, but you're nuts. Your divorce was just final, you've only been an editor for six months so there's that stress and you're settling into a new place. Why bring another headache into your life?"

Nina sighed and sat down. "Speaking of headaches, Jessica gave me a new book to work on. It's worse than the last one."

Charity looked disgusted. "Is she trying to bankrupt that press? She needs to publish something with some oomph in it."

"No, she's doing what her daddy did before her." Nina watched Fred waddle over to them, the couch humiliation evidently forgotten. "She's trying to keep the tradition going."

Charity nodded. "Right into the toilet. She might as well call it the Boring Press."

Nina closed her eyes. "I know it. The whole place is going to fold, and I'll be out of work, and Jessica will kill herself because she's brought the family institution to ruin. And I don't know how to save it, so that depresses me. And I love this place, but it was lonely, and I was coming home so down about work and Jessica, and I just needed something warm to cheer me up." She took a deep breath. "An' that's Fred. He's already cheered me up. Just having him around cheers me up."

Charity watched Fred as his chin sank closer to the floor. "I can see how he'd do that. Peppy little fellow."

Nina ignored her. "And I have a plan for watering him. Come here." She walked to the big window next to her couch and shoved up the heavy old windowpane. "See?"

Charity followed her, and Nina gestured to the black metal fire escape outside.

"The fire escape is only about a foot down from the window." Nina stuck her head out. "This is the third floor, and the back is all fenced-in, and the gate is always closed except on trash day. So I'm going to train Fred to use the fire escape." She pulled her head back in. "Isn't that great?"

Charity nodded, and then patted her arm. "That's great, Neen. It really is."

"Don't feel sorry for me." Nina folded her arms across her stomach. "I've got everything I wanted. I was the one who left Guy, remember? I was the one who got fed up with the high life and living for his career. And it was the right thing to do. I love this apartment, and I love my job. It's just—I get lonely."

"I know." Charity nodded. "It's okay. I know."

"I'm forty," Nina said. "I know this is the prime of my life, I know this is when life begins, I've read all the articles, but I'm forty and I'm alone and—"

"I know." Charity put her arms around her and held her tight. "I know. You're going to be okay."

Nina nodded against her friend's shoulder. "I just wanted somebody to talk to at night and cuddle and watch old movies with. You know? So I got Fred."

Fred waddled back toward them.

"Well, it's a start." Charity let go of Nina and looked at Fred. "What kind of dog is Fred?"

"Part basset, part beagle, part manic-depressive." Nina frowned down at him. "Fred, could you cheer up, please? Look at what a great place you've landed in."

"Yeah, and the best is yet to come," Charity told him. "Wait till you see the fire escape she has for you."

Fred sighed and lumbered on, and they watched him cross the room, his toenails clicking on the hardwood, before Nina said to Charity. "I just need one little favor."

Charity nodded. "Sure."

"Could you baby-sit Fred for me while I go out and buy a leash and food? I'd take Fred, but he sticks his head out the car window, and the wind blows up his nose and makes him sneeze, and the dog snot flies back in the car." Nina looked at Fred with love. "It's pretty disgusting."

"I can imagine." Charity picked up her purple suede bomber jacket. "No, I will not baby-sit this mutt for you. He looks like he's going to end it all at any minute, and I don't want to be responsible if he throws himself off the fire escape." She looked down at Fred with resignation. "Make a list. I'll go get him what he needs. Do they make uppers for dogs?"

"He's not really depressed," Nina told her as she went to find a pad of paper to make the list. "He's just deep. He has deep thoughts."

"Right. Deep thoughts." Charity shook her head again. "Make that list. And while you're at it, add Amaretto and ice cream to it."

Nina stopped her search for paper. Amaretto milk shakes could mean only one thing: a My-Life-Is-In-Trauma party. And with Charity, who ran her life as efficiently as she ran the boutique, trauma could mean only one thing. "Not Sean, too?"

Charity nodded. "Sean, too. How do I do it? How can I live in a city full of men and always pick the rats?"

Nina searched for something comforting to say. "Well, they're not always rats."

"Oh, yeah?" Charity folded her arms. "Name the one who wasn't."

"Well..." Nina searched her memory. "Of course, I didn't know you for all of them—"

"Twelve of them," Charity said. "Twelve guys since I was sixteen, twelve *significant* guys since I was sixteen, twelve guys in twenty-two years, and I can't come up with a winner."

"You're sure it's over?" Nina tried to find a bright side. "Maybe he's just having second thoughts because you're both getting so serious. Maybe—"

"I caught him in bed with his secretary," Charity said. "I don't think she was taking dictation. Not with what she had in her hand, anyway."

"Oh." Nina wrote down Amaretto and ice cream on the list. Amaretto milk shakes might not be the healthiest way to get over a life trauma, but it was Charity's way. Come to think of it, she could use one, herself. "Get chocolate syrup, too," she told Charity. "Let's go for the whole enchilada."

While Charity went shopping, Nina and Fred practiced on the fire escape.

"Come on, you can do this," Nina coaxed him, and together they climbed in and out over the low polished wood windowsill.

Fred was not crazy about the metal staircase, so Nina spread out a rag rug so he'd land on something soft.

On the other hand, he loved the leap from the window.

"Try not to overshoot," Nina warned him, but the fire escape was wide, and Fred was not aerodynamic, so after an hour, Nina was content that Fred would not be plummeting to his death from overexuberance.

She was also sure it was time for Fred to see some grass. "It's a shame you're not a cat. I could just get a litter box," she told him as she coaxed him down the two flights of fire escape with a piece of ham.

Fred whined a little as he eased himself down to the second floor.

"Shh." Nina glanced in the closed window of the second-floor apartment. "I don't know this guy yet. He keeps strange hours. Be very, very quiet here, Fred. We want the neighbors to love you."

Fred shut up and eased himself down another step.

"I love you, Fred," Nina whispered as she backed down the metal stairs. "You're the best."

By the time Charity came back, Fred had done the fire escape twice and was philosophical about it. "We'll take walks, too," Nina promised him. "But this is going to work."

"He can do it?" Charity walked back into the room after putting the ice cream in the freezer and shook her head, amazed. "I wasn't gone that long."

"Fred is very intelligent," Nina told her. "Watch." She opened the window. "Here you go, Fred. Born free."

Fred scrambled onto the box Nina had put by the window to aid his exit. He turned to look once over his shoulder, and Nina nodded.

Then he hurled himself through the window.

"Oh, my God!" Charity ran to the window, Nina close behind.

Fred sat on his rug on the fire escape, looking smug.

"Part basset, part beagle, part kamikaze," Nina said. "We have to work on his takeoff, but he's pretty good, don't you think?"

Charity stepped back from the window. "I think he's great." She smiled at Nina. "I really do. He smells, but he's great."

"Well, that's what I thought, too." Nina watched Fred sway down the fire escape to the backyard.

"Here's the rest of your stuff." Charity handed over the paper bag she'd been clutching. "Your change is at the bottom."

"Thanks, Char." Nina dumped everything out onto her round oak dining table and pawed through it, delighted, stopping only when she found a small jeweler's box tied with a silver ribbon in the middle of the pile.

"That's a baby present," Charity told her. "I'll give you a shower later."

Nina opened the box and took out an oval sterling-silver name tag engraved with Nina's address under a lovely script "Fred Askew."

"Oh, Charity, it's *beautiful*," Nina said.

"Just in case he gets lost." Charity watched as Fred's top half appeared in the window, wobbling back and forth as his toenails scrabbled on the brick outside. "Or stolen."

"I think I'd better put a box outside, too." Nina put the tag down and went to haul him in. "He seems to have a rear-end-suspension problem."

"Among other things," Charity said. "Listen, I've got to go."

Nina put Fred on the floor and straightened. "What about the Amaretto?"

Charity bit her lip. "Can we do it tomorrow night? We both have to work tomorrow morning, and I'm going to need you a lot more tomorrow night since it's a Friday and . . . you know."

Nina nodded. "I know. Fridays are the worst. Sure. That'll be better. You can spend the night."

Charity looked down. "That all right with you, Fred?"

Fred sighed and waddled off.

"He's delighted," Nina said.

"Yeah, I could tell he perked right up," Charity said. "See you tomorrow."

THE PHONE WAS RINGING when Alex let himself into his stuffy second-floor apartment. He answered it, cradling the receiver between his shoulder and his ear as he struggled to put the window up and let a little air into the place.

"Alex?"

Great. Debbie. "Yep, it's me." Alex stuck his head out the window, trying for some fresh night air. The hell with it. He climbed out the window and sat on the fire escape,

taking off his shoes and socks and throwing them back in through the window as he talked. "What's up?"

Debbie's voice was relentlessly cheery. "I thought we might do something tomorrow since it's your birthday. And my sister's kids want to go to the movies, so I thought we could—"

"Sorry," Alex lied.

"Alex, if you'd just *try*—"

"No, really, I'm booked the whole day with my family. One after another the whole damn day."

"Why?" Debbie sounded frustrated. "Why can't they see you all at once?"

"Because they're all trying to talk me into specializing in their areas." Alex flexed his toes in the breeze and felt better. Maybe if he gave up wearing shoes—

"Well, I think they're right," Debbie said. "If you specialized in something else, you'd make more money."

"I have all the money I need." Alex stripped off his white T-shirt while she was talking, so he missed what she said next. "Give me that again?"

"I said, you have loans to pay off. Being in debt isn't bad for a bachelor, but what about when you want to get married and have kids?"

Alex sighed and threw his shirt through the window. "Debbie, we've had this discussion. I don't want kids."

"Well, not right now, but someday you'll want a family and then—"

"I have a family," Alex said. "They drive me nuts. Why would I want another one?"

"A family of your *own*," Debbie said.

"Debbie, you're not paying attention. I don't want kids. Ever."

There was a long silence on the end of the phone, and Alex realized that she'd heard him for the first time.

"I do," she said.

"I know," Alex said. "That's why I've been trying to warn you. I like you a lot. I have a good time with you. But I don't want kids. I don't even want to get married. I've had family up to here. I don't want any more."

"Well." Debbie cleared her throat. "Well, all right. I guess there's not much point in us seeing each other anymore then, is there?"

"Not unless you just want to kick back and have a good time." Alex knew he was supposed to be panicking at her ultimatum, but all he could dredge up was a mild willingness to try again. "We could see some movies. Talk. Just be us together for a while. Get to know each other."

"Alex." Debbie's voice was tight with controlled anger. "We've been dating for six weeks. We know each other. We have seen enough dumb movies and done enough talking. I want a future. I want it all."

"Well, I hope you get it," Alex said cheerfully. "Good luck."

Debbie hung up on him.

Alex put the phone on the windowsill and leaned back against the fire escape again, trying to decide if he was depressed that Debbie was gone. He wasn't. In fact, the only depressing part was that he wasn't depressed. He should be depressed. Debbie was a very nice woman, but he didn't care at all that she was out of his life.

He was a slime. Worse, he was turning into Max.

Still, he'd stuck it out with Debbie for six weeks. That was pretty good. Maybe next time, he'd find a woman who was happy just to be with him, cruising through life and the video store, without a need to produce more family obligations that would make him crazier than he already was.

There was Tricia, for example, the little blonde in the business office. She'd asked him to dinner once, but he'd

turned her down gently because of Debbie. She seemed
nice. Maybe Tricia would be more interested in food and
Casablanca than in planning car pools and country-club
memberships. Maybe he'd call her if he lived through his
birthday tomorrow without being sent to prison for strangling a family member.

The fire escape was cutting into the muscles in his back
so he sat up and stretched and crawled through the window. The couch was close enough to catch a little of the
breeze. All he needed was sleep. With any luck, he'd sleep
through his birthday and not have to see any of his nearest
and dearest before he went back to work on Saturday.

LATER THAT NIGHT, Nina relaxed on her overstuffed couch
with Fred heavy and warm beside her, now redolent of both
the dog shampoo she'd washed him with and the Duende
perfume she'd spritzed him down with on a whim. He'd
been annoyed, but she'd bribed him with gourmet dog biscuits, and he was happy now, sighing in his sleep while she
watched Mel Gibson blow up something on TV.

She had the sound off so she could watch Mel without
having to listen to him, and the traffic rumbled faintly
outside in the May night, punctuated now and then by the
sirens of the ambulances heading for Riverbend General
two blocks away, reminding her that humanity was close at
hand. Best of all, Fred was warm beside her, and for the
first time that day, she felt secure enough to turn her full
attention to her problems. With Fred around, they didn't
seem so bad.

One problem was her job. She'd started as a secretary to
Jessica Howard of Howard Press, a woman whose beige-
suited exterior hid a warm heart and an appreciative spirit,
and within six months Jessica had promoted her to editor.
That was good. Unfortunately, she was editing memoirs of

upper-class stiffs who'd never had an original thought, and
collections of essays by academics on topics so obscure that
even if they were original nobody cared. "Did you ever
think about branching out?" she'd asked Jessica. "Into
fiction? Something popular like romance novels? I hear
they do very well."

Jessica had looked at her as though she'd suggested
prostitution. "Popular fiction? Not in my lifetime. I'll pass
Howard Press on to the next generation as honorably as it
was passed to me."

Nina had repressed the impulse to point out that the press
might not survive Jessica's lifetime. In fact, if the figures
she'd seen while she'd been Jessica's secretary were accu-
rate, Howard Press might not survive lunch. And it was
such a shame. Jessica was a good person who loved books;
she should have a successful press. Unfortunately, Jessica
wouldn't have known a bestseller if it bit her.

Nina cuddled Fred closer. "Want to write a book, Fred?
That dog in the White House made a mint, and she didn't
have near your class."

Fred snored and twitched.

Nina kissed the top of his sweet-smelling head. "I'll take
that as a no."

Her other problem was the loneliness. It had been bad
this last week, being in a new place and being so lonely.
She'd been lonely before in the big house, but she was used
to being lonely there. Her marriage had been a series of
important parties and important charities and important
career moves for her husband, but after the first couple of
years, not much warmth and not much fun. She and Guy
had laughed together at first, but then his future had gotten in their way, and the fun had stopped. That's the way
it was with professional men: they thought they were their
careers and they forgot how to have fun while they built

empires. And she'd been Mrs. Empire, feeling emptier and emptier until she'd finally gotten up the courage to leave Guy, to file for divorce and go looking for a life of her own, hoping for warmth and good times.

He'd been stunned when she'd told him she was leaving. "Why?" he'd said. "I never cheated on you." And Nina, annoyed that he'd missed how empty their lives had become, had said, "Good, I never cheated on you, either." And Guy had said, "Of course not. You're not the type. And now you're going to live the rest of your life alone? You're almost forty, Nina. You're not going to find anyone else at your age. Why don't you go get a facial? That always makes you feel better."

She'd thought he was wrong, thought it would be better once she had a place of her own, but she'd only been in the apartment a week when she'd realized what Guy had been talking about: lonely was lonely, no matter where you lived. He just hadn't realized that it had been lonelier living with him than without him. She gathered Fred to her and put her cheek on his furry little head, grateful to have him with her.

Guy hadn't been the only one who'd pointed out that she was likelier to meet a terrorist than a good man. Her mother had been even blunter. "You're leaving Guy just as your body's going," her mother had warned her. "You've put on weight, you've got crow's-feet and I'm sure you're sagging in more places than just your jawline. This is a mistake. Tell Guy you've changed your mind." And when Nina had said, "No," her mother had washed her hands of her. "Fine. Leave the money and society to be some drab, middle-aged divorcée. It's your life. But don't come crying to me when you realize what you've done."

Even Charity had put her two cents in. "Your mother's an ice cube and always has been. Forget her. But I've got to

tell you, Neen, it's a jungle out there. Guerilla dating. Brace yourself."

Well, she wasn't going to brace herself, because she was not going looking for another man. From now on, she was building her own life and staying as far away from men as she could. She had her career, her apartment, and now she had Fred, too.

Fred stirred again, and Nina held him close. Now she had Fred to come home to, and he was all she was ever going to need. Fred would always love her and would never leave her. "We're going to be together forever," she told him. Then she fell asleep with her arms around him, his snores echoing in her ears.

DEBBIE WAS LICKING wet, sloppy kisses on his face. "No," Alex mumbled. "No, I don't want kids." He tried to push her nose away until somewhere in the recesses of his sleep-fogged mind he remembered that Debbie's nose hadn't been long and furry. Then he opened his eyes and screamed.

There was an animal on the couch next to him.

Alex sat up and the animal rolled off and landed on the floor with a thud.

"What the hell?" Alex turned on the lamp, and the soft light flooded the room and showed him the thing at his feet.

It was a basset hound with all four legs in the air, looking like inflated road kill.

Alex bent down. "Hello?"

The dog rolled over slowly, blinking at him in reproach. This dog was very good at reproach. In fact, this dog could make Hannibal Lecter feel guilty.

"I'm sorry," Alex told him. "You scared me." He scratched the dog behind the ears, and the dog's eyes closed as he gave a little doggy moan. "Where you from, buddy? Better yet, how'd you get in here?"

He looked over at the apartment door: closed shut. That pretty well meant the window. He looked at the dog in disbelief. "You came in the window? What are you, Superdog?"

He walked over and stuck his head out the window. The back gate was shut tight. "You must live here in the apartments."

The dog turned his back and waddled to the door, but Alex caught a glint of metal on his collar before he turned.

"Wait a minute." Alex followed him to the door and bent down to read the tag. Fred Askew, it said. 2455 River Dr., Apt. 3. "You're one floor up, Fred, old buddy," he told the dog as he picked up his shirt, "let's go see if anybody's home."

2

NINA STRETCHED and squinted at the clock on the mantel. Eleven. Time to wake up, put Fred out and go to bed.

Fred?

Fred wasn't next to her anymore. She leaned off the couch to look under the end table, but he wasn't there. Suddenly the apartment seemed too quiet, and she went from bedroom to kitchen to living room calling Fred's name.

He was gone. She'd fallen asleep, and he was gone. She stuck her head out the window and searched the yard anxiously for him.

No Fred.

She crawled out the window and ran down the two flights of fire escape, desperately searching the pavement below for Fred's broken body.

No Fred.

She paced the backyard in the dark, inch by inch, looking behind and even in the Dumpster, just in case Fred had developed aspirations and had managed to climb inside.

No Fred.

The back gate was still locked, and the fence was too high for any dog to have jumped over, let alone the aerodynamically challenged Fred.

Nina climbed back up the fire escape, her throat tight with fear and loss, and crawled through the window, not

sure what she was going to do next. She sank into her big armchair and tried to think.

Call the pound. Call the police. "I've lost my dog. He's part basset, part beagle, part darling."

"Oh, Fred," Nina mourned out loud, and then jumped when someone knocked on her door.

The guy at the door was tall, blond, broad-shouldered and boyishly good-looking, and when she blinked up at him and said, "Yes?" he leaned against the doorjamb, loose-limbed, careless and confident. He nodded at her. "Would you be Fred Askew's mother?" he asked, and then she looked down and saw Fred sitting bored at his feet, his little silver ID tag glinting in the light from the hall.

"Fred!" Nina shrieked and dropped to her knees to gather him into her arms. "Oh, Fred, I thought I'd lost you forever."

Fred slurped his tongue over her face and then struggled to get free of her. Nina let him go and stood up, wiping her hand across her face to get rid of most of Fred's spit. "Thank you." She beamed at Fred's rescuer. "Thank you so much. Where did you find him?"

"He was sitting on my couch when I woke up." He held out his hand. "I'm Alex Moore. I live in the apartment below you."

Nina wiped her fingers on her skirt and shook his hand, a little dazed. "On your couch? He was sitting on your couch?"

"Surprised me, too." Alex grinned at her. "I think he came in from the fire escape."

His grin was a killer, broad and friendly and a little evil, and Nina felt her pulse flutter in response. *No,* she told her pulse and turned to frown down at Fred. "I told you, it's two flights. You have to climb all the way to the third floor, Fred. You can't just pick any window and climb in."

Fred did the dog equivalent of a shrug and walked away.

Alex raised his eyebrows. "You trained him to climb the fire escape?"

Nina bit her lip. "I was hoping no one would notice. I'm sorry. I—"

"No, I think it's great. Weird, but great." He grinned at her again, and Nina was struck once more by how attractive he was. Not handsome or distinguished like Guy. Just comfortably good-looking. Warmly good-looking. Stirringly good-looking.

And he couldn't possibly be thirty yet.

This was a bad sign. It was also understandable since she'd been celibate for a year, but it was still a bad sign. This guy was a child. If she kept this up, she'd be buying a Porsche and cruising the local high schools.

"I can't thank you enough, Mr. Moore," she began and stopped when he shook his head.

"Alex." His eyes went back to Fred. "How long has he been climbing the fire escape?"

"Just since this afternoon," Nina said. "I'm sorry."

"Don't be." His eyes came back to hers, brown and kind and alive with intelligence and humor, and she clamped down on any strange thoughts she might be having. "If Fred hadn't climbed in my window, I wouldn't have met you," he said, "and I think knowing your neighbors is important. Of course, I haven't met you yet. Let's try this again." He held out his hand again. "I'm Alex Moore."

"Oh." Nina took his hand, flustered. "I'm Nina Askew."

"Hello, Nina Askew." His hand was large and warm, and he had lovely long fingers, and Nina pulled her hand away as soon as she realized she was having thoughts about his fingers.

"Hey!" he said, and Nina flinched before she realized that he was looking beyond her. She turned just in time to

see Fred fling himself out the window, and she said, "No, Fred!" as Alex moved past her.

She followed him to the window and watched with him as Fred waddled down two flights of stairs to the backyard where he promptly watered the Dumpster.

"Smart dog." Alex quirked an eyebrow at Nina. "Did you teach him to do that?"

"I taught him the stairs," Nina said. "He already knew how to lift his leg."

"Smart woman," Alex said, smiling into her eyes.

Oh, boy. "Would you like a Coke?" Nina asked and then kicked herself for asking. The last thing she needed was an incredibly sexy underage male drinking Coke in her kitchen.

"Love one," Alex said.

FOR AN UGLY DOG, Fred had a very cute mother.

Once Fred had scrambled back through the window, Alex followed Nina into the kitchen, trying not to admire the swing of her round hips in her wrinkled brown skirt. He was pretty sure she'd just woken up: her short dark curls were rumpled and her big dark eyes were still a little sleepy and her pale pointed face was creased from a pillow somewhere. Pillows made him think of beds, which only led to one thing, and he told himself to knock it off or he'd end up like Max.

Of course, Max was a pretty happy guy.

Alex sat down at the table, trying not to stare at the soft curves in front of him. Very attractive woman, Fred's mother. He owed Fred.

She took two blue-checked mugs from the cupboard and opened the freezer door, automatically putting her free hand up to push the large glass-covered pot on the top of the fridge farther back. Then she scooped ice into the mugs

and nudged the door closed, and Alex admired her effi-
ciency and her arms at the same time.

When she took two cans of soda out of the fridge and put
the mugs and cans in front of him on the round oak table,
he saw her face clearly for the first time, the tiny lines
around her dark brown eyes, the softness in her face. She
was Max's age, maybe a little older. Her face looked settled, not serene exactly, but not the searching, anxious look
that Debbie's face had. She looked wonderful and comfortable and centered in herself, and he wanted to tell her
so, but he stopped in time. She might think it was a pass.

Which it would be, come to think of it, and that would
be a bad idea since she lived right above him, and if she
took offense, there'd be tension whenever they met. And if
she didn't take offense at the pass, she would later when he
explained he didn't want to get married. He had enough
problems; no point in screwing up the only place he could
come to escape.

"Thank you," he said, and she said, "Thank *you* for
bringing Fred home." Then she smiled at him, and he felt
a little dizzy for a minute.

"I'm sorry Fred came through your window," she said.

"I'm not," Alex said. "This way we get to talk. It's a
nice building, and now it's nicer because you're here." She
flushed, and he thought, *not used to getting compliments,
huh?* and wondered if there was a man in her life and if so,
why wasn't she used to getting compliments?

"I haven't met the other people yet." She poured herself
a Coke before she sat opposite him. "Well, I've met the
landlord on the first floor, of course. And I hear somebody go by on the way up to the fourth-floor apartment
sometimes, but I hate to open the door and introduce myself. It seems pushy."

Alex laughed. "The fourth floor is Norma Lynn. She loves pushy. In fact, I think she invented it. She's seventy-five—"

Nina blinked. "And she's on the fourth floor? That's awful!"

"No, it isn't." Alex sat back and watched her outrage. Nice woman. "Norma had her pick of apartments when this place was first chopped up."

Nina seemed confused. She looked good confused, too. "She wanted the fourth floor?"

"Norma is in better shape than you and me put together," Alex said and then thought, *Well, not in better shape than you,* and squelched the thought of the two of them put together. He had to stop hanging around with Max; he was turning into a rat. "She climbs those stairs at least twice a day on her way to yoga and to her self-defense class, which is why, as she will tell you, she has the quadriceps of a sixteen-year-old. She also has an exercise bike that she keeps on the fire escape, which is illegal, but she doesn't care. If you put your head out the window at daybreak every day, you can see Norma peddling away. Norma is going to outlive us all."

"Good for her," Nina said. "Maybe I should take her some tea or something. Does she get lonely?"

"Norma? She plays bridge on Tuesday and Thursday afternoons, teaches piano on Mondays and Wednesdays and holds a readers' group on Friday nights. I know because she's invited me to all of them."

Nina smiled, delighted with Norma, and Alex smiled back, delighted with Nina. "Did you go?" she asked.

"She trashed me at bridge and told me I was tone-deaf at the piano," Alex said. "I haven't faced the readers' group yet. I don't read much."

"Maybe I'll go up some evening," Nina said, and Alex shook his head, hating to mess up such a nice plan but knowing Norma wouldn't appreciate it.

"Don't do it. Rich comes to call in the evenings. Every evening."

"Rich?"

"Her younger man." Alex watched Nina's face flush again and thought how pretty she looked flushed. "He's sixty-two. Norma says most guys can't keep up with her, but Rich has no problem. Of course, Rich also runs the marathon every year and finishes in the top fifty, so he's no slouch, either. They're both great, but I wouldn't drop by there uninvited at night for anything. They like their privacy."

"I'll just have to open my door when she's going by sometime, then," Nina said. "She's not shy, right?"

"Right."

"What about dogs?" Nina looked anxious again. "Will she be upset about Fred?"

"Only if he pees on her exercise bike," Alex said. "Norma's pretty easygoing."

Nina looked down at the pile of bones and skin that Fred melted into every time he collapsed somewhere. "Don't pee on Norma's bike, Fred."

Fred snored.

"I think he's got it," Alex said. "Sharp dog."

"And don't go in Alex's window, either," Nina went on, and Alex said, "Well, let's not get carried away here. I can always use the company."

Nina smiled at him again, warm and serene and welcoming, and he blinked, wondering why he was having such a hard time remembering his place in the conversation. There was no reason for her to be confusing him like this. He was hardly over his relationship with . . . with . . .

Oh, hell.

Nina said, "Are you all right?" and he thought, *Get out of here, Alex, she's fogging your mind*. Who the hell had he been dating? She'd been blond, he remembered that. Time to get out. He stood up and said, "I'm great, but I'd better go now. Thanks for the Coke."

She followed him to the door, thanking him again for returning Fred, while he tried to remember the name of the woman he'd been seeing for six weeks. Why couldn't he remember? It had to be age. He was going to be thirty tomorrow, and already the mind was going. What's-her-name had had a narrow escape; their kids would have done lousy on the SATs, and she was the type who would have cared. What the hell was her name?

"Debbie," he said, and the woman in front of him said, "No, Nina."

He blinked down into her dark, dark eyes, which was how he'd gotten in this mess in the first place. "I know you're Nina, I was just trying to remember the name of my... uh, dog."

"You have a dog?" Nina beamed. "That's why Fred came through your window. Looking for a friend."

"No. Debbie was my... never mind." Alex shook his head. "Anyway, Fred had the right idea. I could use a friend, myself."

She held out her hand. "Well, you've got two upstairs now. We really appreciate you coming to the rescue."

He took her hand, trying to ignore how soft and warm it was while he appreciated her, too. *Knock it off,* he told himself and dropped her hand. "Got to go. See you, Fred," he called back over his shoulder and then he escaped into the hall and down the stairs.

On the way down, he met Rich, looking disgustingly healthy in jeans and a gray-striped shirt that matched the gray in his hair, on his way up to Norma's with a pizza.

"Hello, Alex." Rich punched him in the arm. "Not making time with my woman, are you?"

"Rich, you know Norma wouldn't look twice at me. I couldn't keep up her pace." Alex nursed his bicep where Rich had pounded him. Rich had a mean punch. "I was in three, meeting the new tenant."

"Ah." Rich nodded. "I saw her the other day. Very nice-looking." He squinted at Alex. "She's older than you are."

"You should talk," Alex said.

"No, no, that's good." Rich leaned closer. "Older women know things."

Alex hated to ask, but he had to. "What kind of things?"

Rich raised his eyebrows. "Things. You'll find out." He sighed. "Of course, she's no Norma. They broke the mold when they made Norma."

"I always figured Norma broke the mold because she didn't want the competition," Alex said, and Rich roared with laughter.

"Didn't want the competition. Wait'll I tell Norma. She'll love that one."

"Yeah, and if she doesn't, she'll come down and beat the tar out of me," Alex said, and Rich laughed again and went jogging up the stairs with Norma's pizza.

"Older women, huh?" Alex said to his retreating back, but Rich was too far away to hear.

"I READ AN ARTICLE on menopause yesterday," Nina said to Charity, who was sitting on the oriental rug on Nina's living-room floor, looking elegant and sexy in a black silk catsuit. Nina looked down at her own blue-striped cotton pajamas and sighed. *You are what you wear,* she told her-

self, and went back to the feast that she and Charity had assembled on the floor around them: nonfat pretzels, nonfat potato chips and a blender full of chocolate Amaretto milk shake.

And Fred.

Fred was turning out to be a world-class mooch.

Charity rolled her eyes and fed Fred a pretzel, which he took gently in his mouth, dropped on the ground, pushed with his nose, examined closely, and then, deciding it was exactly like the other three pretzels he'd had earlier, ate. "Don't rush into anything, Fred," Charity told him and then turned back to Nina. "Why are you reading about menopause, for heaven's sake?"

"Because I'm forty now." Nina crunched into a pretzel. "It said that perimenopause starts in the forties."

"Nina, you've been forty for about forty-eight hours. Estrogen deprivation won't start for at least another week." Charity leaned over Nina's blue-striped lap to grab the potato-chip bag. "I can't believe you're torturing yourself like this."

"There was a list of symptoms," Nina went on. "Warning signs. They were awful."

"Hot flashes." Charity nodded. "I get those every time I think of Sean. Only I think it's rage not menopause."

"One of them is that your pubic hair starts to thin," Nina said.

Charity stopped with a chip halfway to her mouth. "I did not need to know this."

Nina nodded. "So I was in the shower last night and I looked, but the thing is, I never paid that much attention before, so I don't have any idea if mine's thinner."

Charity dropped the chip back into the bag. "Nina, honey, you're losing your grip."

Nina stuck her chin out. "I just want to know. I want to be prepared."

Charity shrugged and went back to the chips. "So ask Guy."

Nina shot her a withering look. "Ask my ex-husband to check my pubic hair to see if it's thinned in the year we've been divorced? No, I don't think so."

Charity beamed at her. "Well, there's always Rogaine."

"Thank you very much." Nina slurped up more of her milk shake. "And then there's this thing I'm developing for younger men. I was watching 'Friends' the other night and caught myself wondering what Matthew Perry is like in bed."

"I've wondered that myself," Charity said. "You know, whether he'd stop wisecracking long enough to—"

"Charity, I could have given birth to Matthew Perry."

Charity looked at her with patient contempt. "Nina, Matthew Perry is not a real person. He's an actor. He doesn't count. Now, if you were having hot thoughts about MacCauley Culkin, I'd worry. But Matthew Perry, no."

"He counts," Nina said stubbornly.

"Hell, I think about James Dean and he's *dead*," Charity went on. "That doesn't mean I'm heading for the cemetery with a shovel. Fantasy is not the same as reality. You don't have to feel guilty about it."

"It's happening in reality, too," Nina said. "I met my downstairs neighbor yesterday, and I was thinking about how much fun he looked and what great hands he had, and I swear, he can't be more than twenty-five. It's only a matter of time until I'm cruising the high schools."

Charity sat up straighter, which made her black silk move against her curves. It was a shame there wasn't a man around to watch Charity move, Nina thought. The whole effect was sort of wasted on her and Fred.

Fred was investigating the potato-chip bag.

"Downstairs?" Charity said, pushing Fred's nose out of the bag. "You didn't mention any guy downstairs. Who is he? What does he do? Is he married?"

Nina tried to look quelling. "I told you. He's just a baby."

"I like babies," Charity said. "As long as they're not mine. This could be good. Tell me about him."

Nina glared at Charity and her black silk, a combination that could seduce any man of any age. "You're going to jump my infant neighbor?"

"No," Charity said patiently. "I'm going to talk you into jumping your infant neighbor. If he's not married."

"He's not," Nina said, slumping a little. "At least there was no ring, and he didn't mention a wife."

Charity snorted.

Nina gave her a severe look. "And you're not talking me into anything anyway, so just drop it."

"Is he cute?" Charity asked. "What does he do for a living?"

The image of Alex lounging at her table, broad-shouldered and confident, came to mind, but Nina evicted it at once. "Yes, he's cute. I have no idea what he does for a living. Probably something involving a small hat and French-fry oil. He doesn't look too focused."

"That's *wonderful*." Charity sat back, so enthused she fed Fred a potato chip. Fred ate it cautiously since it wasn't a pretzel. "This is great. Make him your toy boy. If he's got some kind of McJob, you won't end up being a corporate wife, and since he's young, he'll still be interested in sex. This is perfect."

Nina glared at her because the thought was so tempting. "It is not perfect. I'm not dating somebody who's fifteen years younger than I am. I'm not dating again at all, I like

being free and not having to go to stupid dinners and dress up for somebody else's career, but if I was going to start dating again, it would not be this guy.'' She thought again of Alex, loose-limbed and long-fingered in her doorway and way, way too young for her. If she started dating him or, dear God, sleeping with him—she swallowed at the thought—people would say she was in her second childhood. People would look at them on the street and wonder what he saw in her. Guy would sneer. Her mother would roll her eyes. His friends would make jokes about Oedipus Alex. She and Alex would have nothing to talk about. She'd be obsessing over thinning pubic hair, and he'd be playing air guitar.

Worst of all, if she slept with him, she'd have to take off her clothes and her mother was right: her body was forty years old. The whole idea was impossible.

And he wasn't interested in her, anyway. Just what she needed, to start fantasizing about a man who thought of her as a mother figure and who just by existing would make her feel older than she already did. She'd end up literally working her butt off to try to look younger than she was instead of enjoying the freedom she had now. ''It would be too humiliating,'' she finished. ''Not Alex. Anyone but Alex.''

Charity grinned. ''Why not? He's never seen your pubic hair before. He won't notice the thinning.''

Nina sighed. ''And to think you're my best friend.''

''Damn right, chickie,'' Charity said, going back to the chips. ''That's why I'm giving you this great advice. Break the kid's heart. He needs it for the growth experience, and it'll make you feel so much better about the divorce. Trust Aunt Charity. When it comes to romance, she knows. Besides, it'll make Guy crazy.''

Nina shook her head and changed the subject before Charity talked her into something stupid. "Forget Guy. My real problems are not with Guy or the infant downstairs, they're with Jessica."

Charity tilted her head in sympathy. "Poor baby. Is this that boring book you told me about?"

Nina nodded. "Some upper-class twit's prep-school memoirs. I thought the rich were supposed to be depraved, but this guy never even short-sheeted a bed. It is the most tedious stuff I've ever waded through."

Charity picked up her shake and stirred it with her straw. "Seems to me, the idea behind a memoir is to have something to remember."

"Not if you're rich," Nina said.

Charity leaned back, thoughtful. "Now, *I* could write a hell of a memoir. When I think of the trauma I've lived through—" She shook her head in self-amazement and slurped up some milk shake.

Nina snorted. "I should have you ghostwrite this book for this guy. Graft some of your sex life onto his non-life."

"I should write my own book," Charity said. "It's about time I had a career instead of a past."

Nina smiled and fed Fred a chip. That would be one hell of a book: Charity's life between covers, one disaster after another, described the way Charity had described it to her over the years.

Nina stopped smiling. It would be one hell of a book. She looked at Charity. "You're right."

"I'm always right," Charity said. "So why aren't I rich and married and getting great sex nightly?"

Nina leaned forward. "Can you write, Charity?"

Charity looked at her, annoyed. "Of course I can write. I can read, too."

"No." Nina grabbed her arm to get her attention. "I mean, can you write? Prose. Could you write a book?"

Charity blinked at her. "A book?"

"Your memoirs." Nina leaned closer. "I know your breakups must have been awful at the time, at all the times, but you're really funny when you talk about them. Could you write a funny, sexy book about your past love life?"

Charity thought about it for a minute. "I don't know why not. My mom says I write great letters." She met Nina's eyes, her own widening as she absorbed the idea. "Yeah. Sure. In fact, maybe this is what I was meant to do. You know, the first thirty-eight years were just gathering material." She shoved the milk shake away from her. "I could do it like an advice book. One chapter for each guy, with a lesson to be learned each time. It'd be like therapy. Twelve chapters. Would that be enough?"

Nina nodded, thrilled that Charity was interested. "Sure. With an intro and a conclusion, shoot for two hundred, two hundred and fifty pages. Do you think you can do this? Do you think you *want* to do this?"

Charity straightened. "I'm positive. This is a great idea. You think Jessica will publish it?"

She will if I don't tell her what it is until it's done, Nina thought. "Jessica is very supportive of feminist literature," she told Charity. "And this would be a feminist memoir, right?"

"Hell, yes," Charity said. "This is great. Do I get money?"

Nina thought fast. "I need a proposal, nothing too detailed that might confuse Jessica. Just a short outline and a sample chapter, maybe your intro. Then I can go to contract and get you an advance. It won't be much. A thousand tops."

"Dollars?" Charity's eyes widened. "It's a deal." She stood up and grabbed her big black leather bag from the table, annoying Fred who'd been hinting for more chips.

Nina looked up at her, dismayed. "Where are you going?"

"I'm going home to write," Charity said as if it should have been obvious. "I can have that proposal on your desk by Monday if I start right away."

Nina stood and reached out to her, trying to think of a way to calm her down. "Uh, Charity, writing isn't that easy. It takes time. It takes—"

"So I'll have it on your desk by Wednesday. You know, I'm going to love this." Charity had grabbed her coat and was at the door. "This is a *great* idea." She came flying back to hug Nina. "You're the best!"

Then she disappeared out the door, and Nina was left to contemplate the new wrinkle she'd just put in her future. If Charity couldn't write a book, Nina couldn't go to contract, and she'd just lost her best friend of twenty years. If Charity could write a book, but it turned out to be unpublishable by Jessica's standards, Nina had just lost her job. If Charity could write a book, and Jessica through some miracle published it...

...it would be a hit and Howard Press would be on its way into the black and Jessica would love her and she'd be a success.

"And pigs will fly," Nina said and sat back down to finish off the rest of Charity's milk shake. Fred was in the potato-chip bag again, so she pushed him out of it and then absentmindedly ate a chip, trying to think cheerful thoughts. She wasn't sure what she'd started, but she was positive she didn't want to dwell on it or on the impossibly young distraction who lived one floor down, and now she had a whole Friday night all to herself just to dwell on both.

Fred wiped his nose on her leg.

"Hello," she said to him. "I hadn't forgotten you. Want to watch a video? Because no matter how pitiful you look, I am not publishing your memoirs. Not enough sex in your life, buddy." She thought of Alex and his damn fingers. "Or in mine, for that matter." Then she squelched the thought. She was not going to start fantasizing about Alex Moore.

Fred put his paws on her leg and whined at her, so she gave him the last of Charity's milk shake. A scant inch of chocolate and Amaretto couldn't hurt him, and he was so pitiful when he whined. She watched him slurp the last of it, his nose jammed into the glass, and then she stood and threw out the rest of the chips and went back to the table to start on the twit's manuscript.

It was worse than she had remembered, so she was grateful when the doorbell rang. She grabbed her blue seersucker robe and deserted the manuscript with indecent haste, only to feel her heart thump when she opened the door and found Alex leaning in her doorway, this time in a white tailored shirt and navy dress pants, his tie loose and lopsided around his neck.

"Hi," he said slowly and distinctly. "Remember me?"

"Yes." Nina peered at him. He did a little weaving on the doorsill, his eyes bright but half-closed. "Been drinking, have we?"

Alex's laugh sloughed into an exhale. "I don't know about you, but I have. It's my birthday. My whole damn family bought me a drink. One at a time. All day." He frowned at her, as if trying to bring her into focus. "Do you have any coffee? I only ask because you looked like a woman who would have coffee when I was up here last night."

Great. And she'd been thinking hot thoughts about this delinquent all day. God, she was pathetic. Well, somebody had to sober him up. "I have coffee." Nina tied the belt around her robe tighter and stepped back to let him in.

He walked past her and stopped to stare at the papers on the table. "You're working. I don't want to interrupt."

At least he had manners. "It's all right." Nina closed the door behind him. "It's a terrible book. Boring. Turgid."

Alex frowned. "Turgid. He was the Russian, right?"

Oh, terrific. "Not a big reader, I see." Nina pulled out a chair from the table and took his arm to guide him into it. "Coffee coming right up. You sit until it's done."

"I took science courses not lit." Alex took off his tie and threw it on the table. Then he picked up a page from the book and began to read while Nina put a filter in the coffeemaker and poured in the coffee.

Fred wandered over to him, and Nina turned to shoo him away, but Alex said, "Hey, Fred," and leaned down to scratch his ears, and Nina forgave him everything.

Alex was a nice guy. So he wasn't brilliant. Big deal. It wasn't as if she was contemplating a relationship with him; she'd already decided that would be ridiculous. What she needed was a friend, a neighbor. And Alex was nice to her and good to her dog. What more could she want in a neighbor?

Fred looked as if he could want more. He nudged Alex's hand, looking for potato chips, and then collapsed under the table from disappointment when none were forthcoming. Alex went back to reading the manuscript. "This is terrible," he told her when he looked up. "Why is he writing about some dumb American prep school if he's Russian?"

"He's not Russian," Nina said. "You made that up. How much have you had to drink?"

"Well." Alex leaned back in the chair, keeping one hand on the table as if for security. "I had breakfast with my sister—Irish coffee. Then I had lunch with my mother and that's always a strain, so I had two scotches. Then my stepmother asked me out for a drink, and I hate saying no to her, so I had brandy. Then my dad took me out for dinner." He cocked an eye at Nina. "When my father eats, the liquor flows. I'm pretty sure I had three whiskies. Then he had the cab drop me off at home, and my brother was waiting for me with a six-pack." He shook his head. "He just left and I laid down and the whole room sort of swooped and I thought of you. Pour some caffeine down me and I'll leave."

Nina took two blue-checked mugs from the cupboard and put them on the table. "Couldn't you have had seltzer with a couple of them?"

"No." Alex shook his head and then thought better of it. "Ouch, that hurts. I had to have something to drown out the refrain."

Nina sat down, intrigued. "The refrain?"

Alex nodded, this time more carefully. "They all had different verses, but when we got to the chorus, they all said the same thing. 'Time to decide on a career, Alex.'" He put his head down and looked mulish for a moment. "I don't want to decide on a career. I think they're pushing me."

Nina looked at him with disgust. She had the Peter Pan syndrome, sitting right here in her kitchen. She sighed and began to finish the job his family had started. Somebody had to. "Well, Alex, they may have a point. I realize twenty-five or -six seems young, but—"

"I'm thirty," Alex said. "Today. Happy birthday to me. Is that coffee done yet?"

Thirty? Dear Lord, and he still didn't know what he wanted to do with his life? What was he doing now?

Checking IDs? Singing in a rock band? Making sure the fries were hot?

"Coffee?" Alex said again and Nina checked back over her shoulder.

"It's still dripping. You're thirty?"

He gazed at her owlishly. "You thought I was younger, huh? Everybody does. No wonder nobody takes me seriously. And I've got a receding hairline and everything."

Nina squinted at him. "No, you don't."

"Yes, I do." He pulled his hair back off his forehead. "See? It's creeping up on the sides."

Nina leaned closer. "Well, a little. But if you want people to take you seriously, choosing a career would be a better move than flashing a minimally receding hairline."

Alex groaned. "Not you, too. Listen, I'm happy doing what I'm doing. All I need is a cup of coffee and I'll be ecstatic."

"Coming right up." Nina got up and pulled the pot out from under the drip spout, feeling disappointed and stupid. She'd been attracted to him and that had been ridiculous since he was fifteen years younger than she was. Then it turned out he was only ten years younger, which was not as ridiculous although still ridiculous, but now he was also shiftless and evidently not too bright. Turgid as a Russian novelist? Okay, he was drunk, but still, this was not good. She turned to the table and poured coffee into the mugs, watching him reach for his before she said, "Be careful. It's hot."

"Thanks, Mom," he said, and she winced. "I'm kidding," he said hastily. "Dumb joke."

"Probably not." Nina put the pot back on the warmer and sank into her seat. "I'm practically old enough to be your mother."

"Not unless you had a lot more fun in kindergarten than I did," he said, and Nina said, "I'm forty. Two days ago, as a matter of fact."

Alex nodded wisely. "It's those years that end in zero that kill you. Twenty-nine was nothing like this."

"Thirty-nine sucked, too," Nina said. "I got divorced."

Alex winced. "Sorry."

Nina shook her head. "No, it's fine now. I have my own place, and I can do anything I want, and I love it. Last night after you left, Fred and I stayed up and watched *The Great Escape* until one-thirty. You can't do that when you're married. I missed out on a lot of great movies because Guy didn't like it when I stayed up late. I love being single."

Alex blinked. "I watched it, too. Steve McQueen and the catcher's mitt. You like old movies?"

Nina nodded. "And James Garner. James Garner is great in that movie." Then she frowned at him. "Now back to your problem. From the wisdom of my advanced years, I can tell you that waiting too long to start a career is a mistake."

Alex sipped his coffee. "You just starting one now?"

"Going back to one I abandoned sixteen years ago," Nina said. "I got very lucky and found a job in publishing after my divorce, but if I'd stayed at it, people would be working for me instead of me working for them. It took me six months to advance from secretary to assistant editor. One of the editors who has seniority over me is your age. It's hard."

Alex shrugged and sipped again. "Why do you care? Age is irrelevant."

"Tell me that when you're forty." Nina put her mug down. "Come on, let's work on your future. You said you liked science courses in school."

"I said I took science courses in school. I didn't say I liked them." He took another sip. "This is excellent coffee. What kind is it?"

"Don't try to change the subject. What do you like?"

"People. Excitement. Noise. Color."

"Maybe we can get you in with the circus," Nina said acidly. "Concentrate here. I'm trying to fix your life."

"You and my whole family. Why don't we leave my life alone? I *like* my life." Alex drained his coffee mug and then stared into it. "You know, this isn't supposed to work, but I do feel better. Must be the caffeine."

"How are you supporting yourself now?" Nina asked, hoping for a direction to steer him in.

"I'm a doctor." Alex pushed his empty mug toward her. "Could I have another cup, please?"

Nina blinked at him. "You're a what?"

"A doctor. Never mind, I'll get it." Alex got up and stepped over Fred to fill his mug from the pot before he gestured it in her direction. "You want more?"

"No." She didn't want more coffee, she wanted to kill him. He'd known what she'd been thinking and had just played along to amuse himself. Turgid as a Russian novelist. How juvenile of him. Well, he was young, but not that damn young. "Very funny. I want to know why the hell your family isn't happy with a thirty-year-old doctor."

"Because I work in the ER." Alex sat down again. "I like the ER. I have a very short attention span and there's always something going on there to keep me interested. Plus, I get to save lives, which makes me feel good."

Nina nodded and thought about strangling him. "And your family wants you to be what? A lawyer?"

"God, no." Alex looked horrified. "That's my uncle Robert. We do not mention his name." He grew thoughtful for a moment. "Although we do turn to him in times of malpractice suits."

He was being deliberately obtuse, which was his right since she was prying into things that were none of her business. She should just butt out. "I don't get this," she told him. "Explain it or you get no more coffee."

"My mother wants me to be a neurosurgeon," Alex said.

"Why?"

"Because she's a neurosurgeon and I am her only child." Alex sipped his coffee. "This stuff is great. I'm feeling human again."

Nina scowled at him. "I thought you said you had a brother and sister."

"I do. She's an oncologist and he's a gynecologist." Alex stopped. "Oh, you mean, how am I an only child? They're half-sibs. Dad got married three times. We're all only children. It's a real bond."

Nina put her chin in her hand, fascinated. "And your father wants you to be what?"

"A cardiologist, since Stella and Max let him down." Alex drained his coffee mug. "I'm feeling a lot better. Have you got anything to eat?"

Nina stood and got a package of Oreos from the cupboard. Fred perked up and moved nearer to Alex's hand. "Why did they let him down?"

"Stella's mom died of cancer, so Stell fixated on that. Max, on the other hand, chose for aesthetic reasons."

"Gynecology is aesthetic?"

Alex broke open the package and took a cookie. Fred moaned a little and leaned on his leg, so Alex gave the cookie to him and took another for himself. Fred spit the cookie out, looked at it, licked it, nudged it with his nose,

licked it again and then picked it up with his teeth and trotted off to the living room.

Alex watched him and then turned back to Nina. "Gourmet dog. Where was I? Oh, yeah, aesthetic gynecology. Well, as Max pointed out to me just an hour ago, why spend your life looking into the chest cavities of eighty-year-olds when you can look into—"

Nina shut her eyes and leaned back against the cupboard. "I don't want to hear this."

"—the eyes of women who are listening to your every word?"

Nina laughed and then tried to glare at him. "You set me up."

Alex grinned at her and nodded. "Just like Max set me up. I laughed, too. You'd like Max. He's old, almost thirty-six."

"Up yours," Nina said politely.

"And Stell is a little older than you. Forty-two, I think. You'd like Stell, too." Alex's eyes met hers, and she felt her heart thump funny for a moment. *Stop that,* she told her heart.

"Next time they do this," he told her, "you come along to protect me."

I'm not going anywhere with you, sonny, she told him silently, but she wanted to know more, so she said, "And then there's your stepmother. Max's mother, right? What does she want you to be? A dermatologist?"

"No, that would be my cousin Tom." Alex crunched the last of another Oreo. "They'd disinherit me if I did that. I'm supposed to do something invasive not topical. Max's mom is a thoracic surgeon, but she doesn't care what I do as long as I pick a specialty."

"What's wrong with the ER?"

"No status, no fame, no glory." Alex picked up his third Oreo. "Do you have any milk?"

"Skim," Nina said and went to the refrigerator, shoving back the Crock-Pot on the top of the fridge that had inched its way forward as she opened the door.

"Why do you do that?" Alex asked.

Nina slammed the refrigerator door and turned. "Push the Crock-Pot? The top of the fridge is the only place I have to keep it, but the vibration from the motor makes it move forward." She squinted back at it. "I should find a better place, but the cupboards are full."

"It's going to fall on you," Alex said. "Move it."

Nina scowled at him. Just what she needed: an infant doctor giving her orders. "It's fine. Do you want this milk or not?"

Fred had returned by now and sat down with a thump by Alex, his butt hitting the ground like a sack of lumpy lead. He wiped his nose on Alex's pants.

Alex didn't seem to mind.

"Don't beg, Fred," Nina said. "Alex will think you've had no upbringing."

Alex fed him another cookie, and Fred went through the drop, lick, nudge routine again before he picked it up and trotted back to the couch. Alex turned to Nina. "Skim milk. How healthy of you." He got up and rinsed out his coffee mug before he held it out to her. "Thank you very much, I'll take some."

Nina poured his milk. "So what are going to do?"

Alex collapsed into his chair. "I'm going to stay in the ER and just wait them out. They're busy people. Eventually they'll go back to their own lives. Except for Max, but he doesn't give a damn what I do. He's just trying to make sure I don't go for something so high-pressured that I become Dad."

Nina put the milk down on the table. "And that would be bad."

"That would be terrible. My father is a great doctor but a mediocre human being. The only way I'll ever have a real discussion with him is if I develop a heart murmur." Alex crunched into another cookie. "Do you know who raised me? Max's mom, Melanie. My mom left for a residency in Denver, and Dad was too busy, so Melanie just absorbed me into the family with Max and Stella. And Stella wasn't hers, either."

Nina conjured up a motherly thoracic surgeon, surrounded by three adoring children. It was a weird picture. "She must be a wonderful woman."

"Not really. Just efficient and responsible."

That sounded awful. Poor Alex.

Alex straightened a little, and Nina realized her distress must have shown in her face. "Hey, don't knock it," he told her. "When you're a kid, that's pretty good, especially if your own parents aren't around much." He shook his head, remembering. "One day we were all together, must have been a holiday, and I disagreed with something Melanie said, and Dad said, 'Do what your mother tells you,' and Melanie just looked at him and said, 'I'm not his mother.' And Dad said, 'What?' And Melanie said, 'He's Alice's son.' My dad didn't even remember." Alex slouched back in his chair. "Thank God for Melanie. I'd never have made it to adulthood alive and sane." He stopped in the middle of his Oreo, a cautious look on his face, and put his hand on his stomach.

"Well, the sane's still up for grabs," Nina said. "All those Oreos on top of milk, scotch, whiskey, brandy, and beer can't be a good idea. And you call yourself a doctor."

Alex thought about it for a moment and finished the cookie. "I think it was the milk that was the bad idea. But

you need milk with Oreos." He tried to look stern. "It's probably because it's skim milk. Whole milk would have coated my stomach."

Nina tried to look stern back at him. "How old did you say you were? Ten?"

"Very funny." He reached for another Oreo and she moved the package away. "Hey!"

"You've had enough. You're going to get sick."

He frowned at her. "You must be one mean mother."

"Nope," Nina said. "No kids."

Alex sat back. "Did I just put my foot in it?"

"Nope," Nina said again. "Never wanted any. I'm just not the maternal type."

"Now that's interesting." Alex leaned forward again and snagged another cookie while she was off guard. "I never want any, either. Neither does Stella. Max says he gets enough babies delivering them. I've always figured it was our lousy childhoods since we all lost parents. What's your excuse?"

"I'm the oldest of six kids," Nina said. "I already raised five brothers and sisters. I'm done."

Alex raised his eyebrows. "No mom?"

"I have a mother," Nina said, not wanting to discuss it. "She's not interested in children. She gave birth, and then we took it from there."

Alex nodded sympathetically. "Career woman."

"No." Nina took an Oreo from the package, rattling the plastic and alerting Fred, who came to sit beside her. She blinked down at him, surprised by his enthusiasm, and fed him a cookie, and then watched him trot to the couch before she looked back over at Alex. "Not a career woman. Society woman. We had money, we just didn't have parents."

"So you went to college and became an editor?" Alex shook his head. "That doesn't make sense. You're either supposed to become your mother or her opposite."

"I thought that was marry your father or his opposite."

"Same difference. So you became your mother's opposite?"

"No." Nina put down her cookie as the realization dawned. "No, I became my mother. I married a lawyer and did the society thing and became a law-firm wife. My God, I did become my mother." She blinked at Alex. "No wonder the divorce felt so good. That life was hers. Now I'm living mine." She leaned back in her chair. "Boy, does this explain a lot of things." She picked up her Oreo and bit into it, feeling even more liberated than she had before.

"What kind of things?" Alex asked.

Nina stopped in midcookie. "Why do you want to know?"

"Well, I just spilled my family secrets to you," Alex said reasonably. "It's payback time."

"I didn't hear any secrets."

"Okay." Alex nodded at her, the picture of reason. "My father is alcoholic. He doesn't drink before seeing patients but we're keeping an eye on him, anyway. My stepmother kicked an amphetamine addiction a couple of years ago and now is grossly overweight. We worry about her heart. My mother is manic-depressive, and I thank God every day for lithium. My sister has been married three times, all to cardiac surgeons, but refuses to see anything significant in the fact. She is now engaged, at forty-two, to her fourth cardiac man. My brother is chronically single because he lives for the thrill of the chase and finds stability boring, which I have told him is only an overreaction to our tense childhood." Alex shrugged. "Other than that, we don't have

secrets. We're just your standard family of obsessive-compulsive yuppie doctors.''

Nina tilted her head at him. "And what's your secret?"

Alex stirred in his chair. "I don't have any secrets. My life is an open book."

"Bull." Nina got up to rinse out her cup. "You're so defensive you won't talk about yourself. You tell all about your family but you won't say what you want." She turned back to him. "So what do you want, Alex Moore? If you could have anything you wanted, right now, what would it be?"

He sat very still on the chair, his eyes on hers, and she stopped breathing for a moment, sure she saw heat in his eyes, that he wanted her, but that was so ridiculous she shook her head to clear the thought. Then he relaxed. "I want Oreos," he said very seriously. "And I want to be able to come back here and talk when I'm not drunk."

"Sure," Nina said and pushed the package toward him. "Help yourself. Anytime." His eyes met hers again, and she blushed and added, "To the Oreos."

"Right," Alex said. "That's what I thought you meant."

3

"THEN WHAT HAPPENED?" Charity said the next day when Nina had spilled her guts on the phone.

"Then Fred threw up everything, and the mood sort of died." Nina scratched Fred behind the ears as he stretched out next to her on the couch, getting dog hair on her baby blue sweats as he wallowed himself a place beside her. "I got a book out of the library today on how to take care of dogs, and it said never to feed them people food. We could have killed the poor baby feeding him all those Oreos. From now on, Fred eats only dog food."

Fred lifted his head to give her a dirty look, and she scratched him behind the ears again until he relaxed.

Charity, as usual, had a one-track mind. "Does Alex still get Oreos?"

"No." Nina felt the warm little tingle she'd been getting every time she thought about Alex. That was one tingle she was going to get rid of. "Alex gets nothing. I'm staying away from that man."

"Oh, come on, live a little," Charity said. "I admit the doctor bit is a letdown, but he's still ten years younger. That qualifies as toy boy. Go for it."

"You're telling me this based on your years of experience," Nina said.

"No, if I was basing it on my experience, I'd tell you to run like hell. Kenneth was a doctor, remember?"

"Just vaguely," Nina said. "You weren't married that long."

"A year," Charity said. "Long enough to know marrying a doctor was a bad idea. Don't get serious about him. Just toy with him for your memory book."

The thought was attractive, but Nina shoved it aside. "Speaking of memory books, how is yours coming along?"

"It's wonderful," Charity said. "I wrote all night. It was so exciting. I just love this!"

"That's great!" Nina tried to make her voice sound enthusiastic while she prayed that Charity's book would be publishable. "Tell me about it."

"Well, first of all, I guess I should tell you that I'm going to use 'she' instead of 'I.' I just can't write it with 'I.' It's too embarrassing."

"You're using third person," Nina said. "Sure. That's not a problem."

"And instead of using my name, I'm going to use my middle name," Charity went on. "Charity seems sort of... not very serious, you know?"

"What's your middle name?"

"Jane," Charity said. "That's serious, don't you think?"

"Yes," Nina said, beginning to worry that Charity was going to plan forever without ever writing anything. "Did you write any of the book yet?"

"Of course I wrote part of the book." Charity sounded indignant. "I finished the first chapter. It's about Howard." Her voice grew thoughtful. "You know, I'd forgotten a lot of this stuff before I sat down to write it. This is like therapy only much cheaper."

"Howard." Nina frowned, trying to remember. "Was he the hockey player who wanted you to wear the mask and pads?"

"Oh, please." The disdain in Charity's voice was clear over the phone. "That was Helmut. I could barely do a paragraph on him. He wasn't that interesting."

"I found him interesting," Nina said, but Charity plowed on through her.

"Howard was my date to the Riverbend Spring Fling."

Nina sat up, displacing an annoyed Fred. "In high school? You're going that far back?"

"I'm thinking about regressing to past lives. The faraway stuff isn't as painful to write about."

"All right, all right." Nina backed down before Charity could. "The Spring Fling is fine."

"The chapter's called 'Gone With Her Virginity,'" Charity said.

Nina thought of Jessica. "Great title," she lied. "What's next?"

"Mitchell. The Eagle Scout I hooked up with my senior year. We spent a lot of time working on his woodsman's badge."

"Sounds...natural."

"I'm calling that chapter 'Forest Grope.'"

Nina winced. "Catchy."

"And then I'll do that senior fraternity guy I dated as a college freshman," Charity said. "Roger. You knew me by then. Remember Roger, the creep?"

"Vaguely," Nina said.

"I'm going to call that one 'Animal Louse,'" Charity said. "You know, I'm really getting into this."

Nina thought of Jessica and what Jessica would think of Charity's memoir. "Go for it," she told Charity. "But I want to see the first chapter as soon as it's done. Do *not* come to the office and show it to Jessica without me seeing it first."

"No problem," Charity said. "Now it's Saturday afternoon, and you deserve a break. Go downstairs and seduce that nice boy. It'll round off your weekend."

"I'm not going near that nice boy," Nina said. "I don't care what you say. I'm staying in my apartment and watching movies with my dog."

ON MONDAY, Nina came home to find her dog glaring at her.

She put her briefcase on the couch and dropped to her knees beside him. "I know, I know, I haven't been here all day. But Fred, there's more to life than weekends. I *have* to work all day. That's how I get the money to keep you in dog biscuits." She scratched him behind his ears and rolled him over on his back to rub his tummy until he stopped being hostile and went back to morose. "You know what you need, Fred?" she said brightly, and he pricked up his ears, probably hoping to hear the word *Oreo*.

"You need to get out," Nina finished getting to her feet. "Let me change, and we'll go for a walk. A *walk!*"

Since "walk" in no way sounded like "Oreo," Fred remained morose.

"You're going to love it, Fred," Nina said, but fifteen minutes later, when she'd changed into jeans and her old pink T-shirt and hooked his new leash to his new collar, it was clear that Fred was not going to love it.

Nina opened the door and tugged him forward, and he tugged back. "Come on, Fred." Nina tugged harder and Fred lurched a couple of steps closer to the door, still pulling backward. "You're going to like this. Trust me." She tugged still harder, and Fred's feet slid out from under him as his body bumped over the door frame and into the hall.

"Troubles?" somebody said from behind her and she turned to see a tall, gray-haired woman dressed in olive

green cashmere running clothes. She was beautiful in the structure of her bones and the brightness of her eyes, but she was also intimidating. Nina was suddenly conscious of how baggy her own jeans were and how faded her T-shirt was.

And Fred was no help. Nina looked at him, still splayed on his stomach. "I was just taking my dog for a drag," she told the woman. "I'm hoping he'll get the hang of this before we hit the stairs."

The woman laughed and held out her hand, and Nina wasn't intimidated anymore. "I'm Norma Lynn from upstairs."

Nina took her hand. "I'm Nina Askew. And this—" she dropped her hand and gazed down at Fred with disgust "—this is Fred."

"Hello, Fred," Norma said, and Fred got to his feet and walked the four steps he needed to be within smelling reach of Norma's Nikes.

"I've been neglecting him," Nina told Norma. "This is a guilt walk."

"It's not good to neglect males," Norma agreed. "They're such babies about it, and they sulk. It's why I'm never living with another one of them. No offense, Fred."

"I couldn't agree with you more," Nina said. "Except for Fred. All he needs is his ears scratched and some Oreos and he's happy." She looked at the morose-as-usual Fred. "Well, he's content."

"You could keep a lot of men content with that," Norma said. "Although it may take you more than that to keep Alex cheerful. Very physical young man, Alex."

Nina blushed and then kicked herself for blushing. "Alex and I are just friends."

Norma shook her head. "Too bad. He seemed very taken with you when he told me about you yesterday." She looked

at Nina sharply. "An excellent young man, Alex. No bluster and a very good sense of humor. You could do a lot worse."

"He's ten years younger than I am," Nina blurted before she remembered that Norma had thirteen years on her Rich.

"Yes," Norma said. "Isn't that nice? He won't die and leave you a widow or run out of steam in bed while you're hitting your stride." She smiled at Nina, serene and lovely. "Don't let foolish assumptions about what's appropriate keep you from a good man. There are too few good men around to ignore one just because he's the perfect age for you." She patted Nina's arm. "But of course, it's your choice. I'm so glad we've met. You must come out running with me someday. Bring Fred."

At the sound of his name, Fred stood up again and whined a little.

"There, see?" Norma smiled down at Fred. "He wants to run."

"I've never seen Fred run," Nina said.

"Then that will be something else new for you." Norma turned to the stairs. "Broaden your horizons. They're the only ones you'll ever have, so make the suckers as wide as possible." And then, while Nina watched, Norma ran up the stairs, her quadriceps straining against her cashmere sweats. They were damn good quadriceps.

"Maybe if I had quadriceps like that," Nina told Fred. "And maybe if he was ten years older, maybe then I'd jump Alex. But with this body, no."

Fred sat down again.

"Come *on*, Fred," Nina said and dragged him toward the stairs. "We'll both run a couple of blocks. Then we'll have an Oreo. *One* Oreo."

At the magic word, Fred rose to his feet and clambered down the stairs under the delusion that he was heading toward cookies. Nina didn't care; at least they were moving toward a new experience.

After meeting Norma, she was pretty sure she was going to feel guilty if she didn't turn up with a new experience on a regular basis from now on.

LATER THAT EVENING, Alex had an old experience.

"It's time you made a decision, son," his father blustered at him over the phone, and Alex tried to listen while he put on his socks with one hand and checked his watch. He was due to pick up Tricia for dinner in fifteen minutes, and he still didn't have a tie on, not to mention a jacket or shoes. He hated ties and jackets. He wasn't too crazy about shoes, either.

"Alex?"

"I'm listening," Alex said, "but it's pretty much too late now." He stood up and rifled through his drawer looking for a tie. "All the slots are filled. I couldn't—"

"That's what I called about," his father broke in. "We have an opening in cardiology. Young Lutin dropped out of the program. Went to Tahiti to paint. Tahiti! What kind of fool would give up an important career to paint in Tahiti?"

"Gauguin." Alex stared sightlessly into his top drawer, envying Lutin who would never have to discuss cardiology with his father again.

"What?" his father said, and Alex said, "Nothing."

"It's yours, son," his father went on. "All you have to do is take it."

Oh, hell. "Dad, it's not a good idea to give your son the only opening in the unit. People will notice that you're playing favorites."

"Nonsense. The whole damn hospital knows about the work you do in the ER. You can go anywhere. They know that."

I don't want to go anywhere, Alex thought. *I like the ER,* but his father rumbled on.

"It's time you built a life, Alex. Got married. Settled down. And a wife isn't going to put up with the ER as a career."

As if you'd know, Alex thought, and repressed the urge to point out that being a cardiologist hadn't done much for his father's three attempts at marital stability. "I'll think about it, Dad," he said. "But I've got to go now. I have a date."

"Debbie? Fine, fine girl. She'll make you a good wife, Alex. And a good mother for your children. Don't screw up this time."

Alex picked up a tie and sank back onto the bed. "I already did," he said as he threaded it one-handed around his neck. "Debbie and I decided we'd be happier if we weren't dating. I'm taking Tricia Webster to dinner."

As usual, his father was fast on the recovery. "The little blonde in the business office? Seems very responsible. And sweet. Make you a good wife. And a good mother for your children."

Alex shook his head. His father wasn't going to rest until Alex was a married cardiologist with offspring. At this point, he could introduce him to Fred and his father would say, "Seems very loyal. Make you a good wife. You can adopt."

Thoughts of Fred led to thoughts of Nina. Now, she *would* make a good wife. She was pretty and warm and kind and she kept Oreos and milk on hand and she had a great dog.

And a great body. The thought sprang to mind unbidden, and Alex stopped fighting with his tie and closed his eyes and thought of her, round and warm in her kitchen, laughing up at him with that soft pink mouth, and the memory fogged his mind and made his breath come quicker. He wanted to be taking Nina to dinner, not Tricia, but he knew better than to ask. She was used to older men, successful men like her ex-husband, the rich lawyer. She was used to big bucks and caviar, and he was med-school loans and Oreos.

Of course, if he became a cardiologist, he'd have big bucks and caviar.

His father's voice broke the thought. "Alex, are you listening to me?"

"Yeah," Alex said. "Believe it or not, I am." He must be losing his mind. He needed a better reason for becoming a cardiologist than trying to get a date. Then thoughts of Nina clouded his mind again, Nina sitting across her big oak table from him, her chin in her hand, shaking her head at him, arguing with him, leaning back and smiling lazily at him. He remembered how graceful her neck had been as it curved into the loose pajama top, and how he'd wanted to draw his finger down that curve and pop her pajama buttons, one by one...

There were worse reasons to become a cardiologist.

"Alex?"

"Yeah, Dad. Let me think about this some more."

"Well, don't take too long. I can't hold on to this appointment forever."

"Right," Alex said, bemused with visions of holding on to a naked Nina. "I really am going to think about it."

NINA'S PHONE RANG at ten that night while she was struggling with the final chapters of the upper-class twit's memoir.

"Uh, Nina?" Alex's voice sounded harried. "Could you come down here? I need some help."

"Help?" Nina swallowed. Alex's voice made her first grow tense and then grow warm, which wasn't good. She shouldn't see him. She thought about telling him she was busy, but there was panic in his voice, and if she could help, she should be neighborly...

Five minutes later, Nina was in Alex's apartment, sitting on the couch and patting his weeping date, a tiny blonde with an enormous capacity for loud sobbing, who made Nina feel fat and sloppy in her jeans and pink T-shirt.

"Meet Tricia," Alex said, and Tricia wailed louder, dripping tears onto her flowered slip dress no matter how fast Alex passed her Kleenexes.

"What did you do to her?" Nina asked him, trying not to notice how great he looked in dress pants and a tailored shirt again, even with his shirtsleeves rolled up and his tie loose. Really, he cleaned up *very* nicely.

Alex glared at her. "I didn't do anything to her. I took her to dinner. I showed her a video." Nina narrowed her eyes and he added, "*Young Frankenstein.* Get your mind out of the gutter. Then I kissed her. That's it. I swear to God." He crossed his arms in front of him, looking disgusted with her and Tricia, and his forearms flexed, and Nina lost her train of thought. He had great arms. He had great everything.

And all of it was too young for her.

"He's never going to marry me," Tricia wailed.

"Marry you?" Nina blinked at Alex. "How long have you been dating?"

Alex checked his watch. "We're at the three-hour mark now."

"This is your first date?" Nina stopped patting Tricia. "I'm missing something here."

Tricia looked up at her, her face a sodden mask of misery under her riot of blond curls. "It's all my fault. I told him I wanted to sleep with him. And now he'll never marry me."

Nina raised an eyebrow at Tricia, trying to ignore the spurt of dislike she felt for her. "Gee, I'd think that'd be a good line to take with him."

Tricia shook her head, snuffling. "He said no. He said no!"

Irrationally cheered, Nina looked at Alex who looked as if he wished he were dead. "Tricia enjoyed the wine at dinner," he said in a pathetic attempt at tact.

"And now he thinks I'm a drunk, too," Tricia wailed.

"Well," Nina said, patting faster as she tried to think of a way to convince Tricia to stop crying.

"And I really want to marry a doctor," Tricia finished wetly.

Nina stopped patting again and glared at her. How could anybody look at Alex and just see his medical degree? Even aside from the fact that he was gorgeous, he was also sweet and funny and . . . *Shut up,* she told herself. *Don't do this to yourself.* She stood up. "Well, I think it's time we all called it a night. Alex is going to take you home now. Go get the car, Alex."

"We'll all go," Alex said. "Fred needs the fresh air."

"Who's Fred?" Tricia said. "Is he a doctor?"

Half an hour later, with Tricia deposited at her door, Nina was still fuming. "I can't believe she was going out with you because she wants to marry a doctor."

Alex grinned at her, relaxed behind the wheel now that Tricia was just a soggy memory. "Well, face it—the women I date are not going out with me because of the fancy places I can take them to. I'm an ER specialist with about ten years of loans to pay off. I'm poor. So they plan for the future."

Nina frowned at him, trying not to appreciate the careless way his fingers draped over the wheel, and the way his long body lounged in the seat. Carelessly confident, that was Alex. Not a focused bone in his body. *Don't think about his body.* She tried to find her place in the conversation. "Women should be going out with you because you're terrific."

"Thank you," Alex said. "I'll tell them you said so."

In the back seat, his head hanging out the window, Fred snorted the wind out of his nose.

"Who asked you?" Alex said to him.

"I can't believe she'd be so mercenary," Nina fumed on, grateful to have something to distract her.

"Oh, come on," Alex said. "Why'd you marry Guy the Stiff? Because he was a rich lawyer, right?"

"No, because he was the first man I ever slept with," Nina said. "I was raised strict."

Alex was silent for a moment. "So, how many guys have you slept with?"

"One. Guy." Nina laughed shortly, embarrassed by her lack of an interesting past.

"Okay, smartass, how many *men* have you slept with?"

"I told you," Nina said. "One. Guy. I met him in college and slept with him, and as far as I was concerned, that was it."

Alex turned to stare at her in the dim light of the front seat. "You're kidding."

"No." Nina frowned at his incredulity. He probably thought she was dull and frumpy. Well, the hell with him. So she didn't have much of a past. That didn't mean she wasn't going to have a terrific future. Don't make assumptions, Norma had said. Norma was right. She didn't need to give up men entirely; she just had to give up marrying them. "I was backward then, but I'm not anymore," she told him and stuck her chin out. "I'm going to have an affair." It was a brand-new idea, but with Alex beside her, it sounded like a good one.

Alex didn't look impressed. Or happy, for that matter. "With whom?"

"I have no idea." Nina leaned her head back as the cool night air rushed in her window. She half closed her eyes and tried to look mature and depraved. "I'm still looking."

Alex grinned at her. "Well, put me on the shortlist."

Hello. Nina swallowed. He was kidding. If she took him seriously and made a pass at him, he'd be embarrassed. Look at how he'd been with Tricia. "Very funny," she said and changed the subject. "I can't believe Tricia was dumb enough to think that offering to sleep with you would turn you off."

"No, she was right about that." Alex turned the car into the alley behind the apartment house and backed it into his parking space.

"What?" Nina stared at him, disbelieving.

"I wouldn't want somebody who would sleep with me on the first date." Alex turned off the ignition. "I have some standards."

"Oh." Nina tried to digest this. It was a *damn* good thing she'd decided not to make a pass at him. Not only would he have thought she was too old, he'd have thought she was too easy. She regrouped. "Well, that's good. I suppose it shows moral fiber on your part that you turned her down."

"I turned her down because she was drunk," Alex corrected her. "If she'd been sober, I'd have slept with her."

"But you just said—"

"I wouldn't have asked her out again, but I would have slept with her." Nina glared at him and he shrugged. "Hey, I did not seduce her. In fact, I was trying to sober her up. I have cups of coffee on my table upstairs to prove it. But if she's going to make an offer while of sound mind, I'm going to take her up on it, or *I* wouldn't be of sound mind."

"Did you ever think of showing some moral restraint?" she asked him icily.

"No," Alex said. "I'm male."

He certainly was. That was the problem. She was sitting next to him in a dark car, and he was the most masculine male she'd been with for a long time. Forever, actually. And she should be angry with him for saying he would have slept with Tricia if she'd been sober, but it was hard to be angry and turned on at the same time, and the fact was, whenever he came around, she got a nice little buzz going that didn't fade until he was long gone.

This was bad.

Get out of this car, Nina told herself and opened the door. "I'm going to let the next one cry all over you." She climbed out of the car and opened the back door for Fred. "Stay away from him, Fred. He's a bad influence on you."

Fred gathered himself together and leaped for the ground, staggering a little on impact.

"Hey, wait a minute," Alex said to Nina, but she was already leading Fred through the gate into the backyard, and there was no way she was going to stop and continue the conversation.

The last thing she needed to do was discuss sex with Alex Moore.

"WHAT DO YOU DO when a woman you want shows no interest in you?" Alex asked Max the next day in the hospital cafeteria.

Max looked at him with contempt over his eggs and hash browns. "That never happens."

Alex pushed his own plate away. "I don't think I'm . . . sophisticated enough for this woman. I think she's used to rich, older guys. I think she thinks I'm a kid."

Max shoved his fork into his breakfast. "You been wearing that beanie with the propeller again?"

Alex frowned at him. "I'm serious, Max."

Max raised an eyebrow, distracted from his food for a moment. "You? Serious about a woman?"

Alex thought about it. "I don't know. Probably not. I'm definitely serious about getting her into bed."

Max nodded and went back to his eggs. "That's more like it."

Alex shook his head. "But it's not going to happen."

Max shook his head and spoke around bites of egg and potato. "You don't know that. Spend some time with her. Charm her socks off. Be debonair."

"Oh, yeah." Alex leaned back. "Debonair. That's the real me."

Max shrugged. "Well, you're the one who said she thought the real you was a Boy Scout."

Alex stared blankly across the crowded cafeteria, thinking about Nina and how Nina had looked in the dark front seat of his car, how Nina's perfume had come to him faint and erotic in the dimness, how Nina's skin had gleamed when they'd passed a streetlight. She'd been so warm and so close . . .

"The thing about Nina," he told Max when he'd come back to earth, "is that when I'm with her, I forget every-

thing but her, so I can't pretend to be somebody else. The only person I can be with Nina is me."

Max froze, his fork poised over his plate. "Don't talk like that. It sounds serious."

"It's not serious," Alex said. "She's just my neighbor. It's no big deal."

"Right." Max pointed his fork at him. "You be careful, boy. Stay away from her."

"Right," Alex said, wondering if Nina liked videos and what excuse he could use to invite himself up to share her VCR.

IN THE NEXT TWO WEEKS, Nina finished editing the twit's memoirs and two books of literary criticism, gave Charity a contract for a book described as "a feminist memoir" and spent six amazingly pleasant and comfortable nights watching old movies with Alex on her TV.

"You get better reception than I do," Alex had told her the first night. He'd knocked on her door and handed her a gallon of skim milk and a large package of Oreos. "You don't mind, do you?"

And she'd said no because she didn't mind at all. In fact, she was flat out delighted even though she'd warned herself not to be. There was something warm and right about Alex sitting on her floor, his back propped up against her couch, Fred draped over his lap thinking intense Oreo thoughts, while people screamed and laughed and cried on the screen in front of them. She'd taken to curling up on the couch behind them, watching the movies over Alex's shoulder, absentmindedly reaching for the cookies or pretzels in his lap while she rediscovered old movies she'd loved like *Real Genius* and *Avanti* and *American Dreamer*.

And sometimes when the movie was over, they just talked, first about the movie and then about other things.

Alex talked about the ER and his family, how much he loved his work and the good times he had with his brother, Max, and Nina told him about the troubles at her work, Jessica and the twit's memoirs and Charity and her book.

Alex had been incredulous when he'd first heard of the project. "She's writing a book about her dates?"

"Charity doesn't have dates," Nina told him, reaching over his shoulder for pretzels, trying not to inhale the scent of his soap on his skin. "She has disasters with cab fare. Like this guy Carlton, the grad student she dated when she was a sophomore. He was really anal retentive about relationships. Charity said even sex had to be by the book."

"What book?" Alex straightened with interest. "There's a book?"

"She calls that chapter 'Sex: The Cliff Notes.'" Nina wanted to reach out and pull him back against the couch, closer to her. Dumb idea. "Jessica's going to go cardiac when she reads the chapter titles."

Alex collapsed back against the couch. "Don't say 'cardiac.'"

"Then there's chapter five," Nina went on, happy again now that he was close. "Wilson. He had an impotence problem."

Alex shook his head. "Don't say 'impotence.'"

Nina reached for another pretzel. "She called that chapter 'Try Hard and Try Harder.'"

"Ouch." Alex winced. "Your friend has a mean streak."

Nina frowned, the pretzel still in her hand. Charity's chapters were a little harsh. In fact, some of them were downright bitter, but they were funny and sexy, so she'd told Charity that it might be a good idea to lighten things up as the book went along so the reader got the feeling that Jane was making progress and that things were getting better for her. Charity had seemed doubtful, so Nina hadn't

pressed the point. The last thing an author needed to hear while she was writing her first draft was criticism.

"I'm sure she'll lighten up in the rewrite," she told Alex. "And chapter six is pretty funny. It's about Ron, this traveling salesman she dated."

Alex closed his eyes. "Let me guess. He slept around."

Nina nodded. "Around forty-eight states. She's calling his chapter 'Mobile Dick.' We're going to have to change that one."

"I can't wait to meet Charity," Alex said. "She sounds like a real sweet woman."

Jessica was interested in Charity, too.

"So tell me about Charity's book," she said to Nina one day in June over lunch. Jessica, as always, looked beige and polished and upper-class. She was the only woman Nina had ever met who had naturally beige hair. They were in Jessica's equally beige office, eating yogurt and kiwi and discussing the changes that would have to be made to the twit's memoir, when Nina had remarked that at least the feminist memoir Charity was working on wouldn't be boring. Jessica had perked right up. One of the many good things about Jessica was that she wasn't elitist or prudish. It didn't bother her in the slightest that Charity ran a boutique instead of a college English department or that she was writing about her sex life.

"It's a history of the changing roles of women," Nina had told her when she'd gone to contract on the book. "An anecdotal, oral history of the sexual revolution."

"Wonderful," Jessica had said and okayed it without reading the proposal. "I trust you," she'd told Nina, and Nina had felt a stab of guilt even though what she was doing was best for Jessica and Howard Press.

"Charity's book?" Nina said now. "She's more than half finished. Seven chapters on the varying expectations of

sexual roles in high school in the seventies and college and young adulthood in the eighties. It's fascinating. Chapter seven is on her first working experience."

Jessica raised a plucked beige eyebrow. "Harassment?"

Nina frowned. "Sort of. Her boss seduced her, and then she found out he was a sexual compulsive."

Jessica's eyes widened. "Fascinating. Horrible, but fascinating."

"Right," Nina said, omitting to tell her that Charity called this chapter "He Was On Fire When I Lay Down On Him."

"It wasn't really harassment," Charity had told Nina. "Presley just never thought about anything else. He probably had sex with his desk drawer when I wasn't around. I finally had to get another job just so I could get some sleep."

"It's going to be an interesting book," she promised Jessica. "A real money-maker."

"That's not what Howard Press is about," Jessica said, but Nina could see the hope flare in her eyes. Jessica needed a money-maker soon, which meant Nina did, too, if she wanted to keep her job.

"It's more than just a money-maker," she reassured Jessica. "It'll make women everywhere rethink their sex lives."

It was certainly making Nina rethink hers. Whatever other problems Charity's book had, her sex scenes were dynamite. As Nina worked her way through Charity's explicit, erotic chapters, the year she'd been celibate began to feel like ten. And Alex wasn't helping things any. She was dreaming about him now, lovely sexy dreams of his hands and his mouth and his wonderful, long body. She'd seen that body in action the night before, when he'd come by and coaxed her out to go jogging after work. Fred had

trotted along between them, disgusted, while they'd laughed and she'd watched Alex move. She thought longingly of the days when she'd lusted after Matthew Perry, safe on the other side of the television screen. Alex was just one flight down, entirely too real, entirely too young.

Not dating was not working. She was going to have to do something.

Two weeks later, after a dozen more frustrating nights with Alex and Ted Turner's video library and at least that many frustrating jogs in the park, she did something.

"I have to start dating," Nina told Charity. She'd gone downtown on her lunch hour to the boutique that Charity managed, and there, in the middle of a lot of red suede, purple spandex and black lace, she came clean. "I'm interested in Alex," she said as they leaned against a display case full of silver chains. "*Really* interested. But it's just because he's the only man I see." Charity opened her mouth, and Nina hurried to cut her off. "And Alex isn't my only problem. Guy is calling again. He wants to have lunch and dinner and sex."

"He asked you on the phone to have sex?" Charity said, intrigued.

"No, but it was in his voice," Nina said. "And when I said I wasn't interested, he pointed out that he knew I wasn't dating because the only other man I ever talked about when he called was the kid downstairs. I need to get out more, rev up my image, see some other men. *Help* me."

Charity frowned at her. "You want me to fix you up on a date."

"No." Nina sat down on one of the little black-enameled chairs that dotted Charity's domain, depressed. "I have a date."

Charity dropped into the chair beside her. "You're kidding."

Nina gave her an exasperated glare. "No. Is it so impossible that I'd have a date?"

"Yes," Charity said. "I thought there for a while you were trying to grow your virginity back. Who is this guy?"

"His name is Michael Thackery," Nina told her. "I edited his memoirs, which are the dullest thing I've ever read, and he came in to the office today to talk about the line edit and asked me to dinner. And I thought, *well, it's a start.* But now I need some help."

"Wait a minute." A grin spread across Charity's face. "This is the *twit* we're talking about, right?"

Nina glared at her. "Charity, this isn't funny. I need *help.*"

"Right. Sure." Charity stood up. "Well, first of all, you have to stop wearing those blah colors. Gray and black do not suit you." She moved around the shop, gathering up red lace and redder cashmere before she came back to Nina. "Here, go try these on."

Nina looked doubtfully at the clothing in her hands. At least there was no red feather boa. "What is this stuff?"

"Red cashmere scoop-necked sweater," Charity said. "Red lace panties. Red lace Incredibra."

Nina fished the bra out of the pile draped over her arm. "This thing is an Incredibra?" The bra dangled from her hand, round and shapely without her. It practically had cleavage without her. "I've heard about them, but I've never seen one."

"Yeah. It sort of pushes everything together and then shoves it up." Charity shook her head. "I tried one on once, but since I'm a C-cup to begin with, it just made me look like I had a very large double chin with a cleft in it. My customers who are B-cups swear by it."

Nina glanced down at her own B-cups. "Okay, I'll take it."

Charity frowned at her. "Don't you want to try it on?"

Nina shook her head. "I'm on my lunch hour. I'll just trust you."

Charity shrugged. "Well, bring back what doesn't look right, and we'll try something else."

That afternoon after work, Nina tried on the clothes, while Fred sat bored at her feet, waiting for his walk. The Incredibra lived up to its name, incredibly bright red and incredibly structured so that her breasts moved up nearer her chin than she thought possible, creating cleavage that was clearly impossible. Combined with the red cashmere sweater, the outfit made Nina look like a very good time. *I wonder what Alex would think of this,* she thought, and then stamped on the thought. Alex was never going to see her red-cashmered cleavage.

On the other hand, Michael was.

She studied herself in the mirror, not sure she wanted red-cashmered cleavage with Michael. Michael looked as though he hadn't had a sexual thought in his life, but maybe he came alive at night. Maybe incredible breasts were not a good move in Michael's case. Maybe nondescript was better for a first date. No sense promising what she had no intention of delivering.

She stripped off the sweater and the Incredibra, dropping them both on the bed, and started for her dresser to get a regular underwire. Fred put his paws on the bed, grabbed the bra and trotted to the door, and Nina ran after him and grabbed it back.

"Just like a guy," Nina said to him and tossed the bra farther up on the bed as she went to change.

The regular underwire was much better, and the blue sweater she put over it was pretty without being a come-on, and her black skirt was knee-length, no slit. The outfit made her look attractive and responsible. It in no way said,

"Yo, come jump my bones," which was the message Charity said a good date outfit should send. The last thing Nina needed was a good date outfit that sent messages. The Incredibra was definitely going back ...

Nina looked at the bed. The Incredibra was gone.

"*Fred!*" She took a quick lap through the apartment—kitchen, bathroom, living room—and stopped in front of the open window. Fred had found his own way of paying her back for putting off his walk. "You're in big trouble, Fred," she said and climbed out the window.

She spotted him down beside the Dumpster, the bright red bra in his mouth. "*Fred!*" she yelled again, and he ducked behind the Dumpster. "You're dead meat, Fred," Nina told him as she ran down the fire escape. "You're yesterday's news, boy."

She trapped him behind the Dumpster, so he crawled farther behind it, into the cavern made by the open lid against the brick wall. She got down on her hands and knees and peered into the cave and saw Fred sitting there, morose as ever, her Incredibra at his feet.

"Give me that," she said to him. "Right now." She crawled a little way under the lid, and Fred lowered his head and growled at her.

Nina stopped. "You're *growling* at me? You're growling at *me?*"

"Let me guess—De Niro," Alex said from behind her, and she straightened in surprise and banged her head on the Dumpster lid.

"You're going back to the pound," she told Fred as she backed out, rubbing her head.

"Is your head all right?" Alex said when she was standing. "Let me see." His hand was firm against her cheek, tilting her head down so that all she could see was the clean white T-shirt stretched across his broad chest. It was an ex-

tremely good chest, but she'd already been staring at it with lust for five weeks, so she closed her eyes to keep her concentration and to keep from grabbing him. He explored the incipient bump on the back of her head, and she drew a deep breath as his fingers moved through her hair and sent inappropriate chills down her spine. If she leaned forward another inch, she could lick his neck.

That would be bad.

Alex tilted her head back up to him. "The bump's not too bad. We can still go jogging." He let go of her chin and rested his hand on her shoulder. "I saw you streak past my window. Why are you down here braining yourself on a Dumpster?"

"Fred," Nina said, trying hard not to visibly enjoy his hand on her. "He's going through a Stage. It's the Terrible Twos. Or in his case, the Terrible Fourteens."

Alex let go of her and stooped down on his haunches to peer behind the Dumpster. "Fred? What's wrong with you? Get out here."

Fred came trotting out and dropped the bra at Alex's feet.

"The hell with the pound," Nina told Fred as she snatched for the bra. "I'm going to kill you right here."

Alex was too quick for her. He stood, holding the bra by one end, and squinted to read the tag. "The Incredibra." He raised an eyebrow at Nina. "I've heard of these, but I've never seen one."

"Well, now you have." Nina made another grab for it, but he moved it out of her reach again.

"I mean, I've never seen one on an actual woman," he explained. "In the flesh. It's probably something I should experience. For my professional advancement." He smiled at her encouragingly, and it took all of Nina's self-control not to smile back and leap on him.

He was a rat. He was waving her bra around in public. He was gorgeous and she wanted him.

"You want me to model my underwear for you for your professional advancement," Nina said, trying not to think about it.

"It's all right." Alex stopped smiling and made a pathetic effort to look serious and adult. "I'm a doctor."

"I'm going to take you back to the pound with Fred," she told him. "You're both completely untrainable." Then she snatched the bra out of his hand and went back up the fire escape before he could talk her into taking off her clothes right there in the courtyard.

She was going to have to do something about the effect he was having on her. She was going to have to think of something later, when she was calmer. Like when she was with Michael. She'd definitely be calmer then.

"You're never going to see an Oreo again," she told Fred when he followed her back through the window. "Never."

4

SIX HOURS LATER, at what Nina prayed was the end of her date with Michael, she was abysmally grateful she'd passed on the Incredibra for the evening.

Now if she could only pass on Michael.

It wasn't that he was awful. He was just intense and boring, his black eyes so sharp and his gray suit so well pressed that he looked like an eager beaver while he talked like a drone. It was a bad combination, and she wanted away from it, but somehow he'd managed to get himself into her apartment, and although she'd had the good sense not to offer him a drink, she was at a loss as to how to get rid of him. Even Fred was annoyed with him.

Michael had started the evening by staring at Fred and saying, "What is that?" and when she'd told him Fred's name, he'd said, "Good doggy." Fred had given him a look that up till now she'd only seen him use on generic dog food. Things went from bad to worse when they went to dinner and Michael talked about his book. Then they went back to her apartment, and Michael continued to talk about the book while Nina bustled around trying to look busy, opening the window for Fred, straightening the paperwork on her table, yawning, and finally looking at her watch. Nothing seemed to sink into Michael's thick head. Even Fred gave up staring at Michael and strolled off someplace else to amuse himself.

The knock at the door half an hour later came as a welcome reprieve. "Just a minute," Nina told Michael while he was in midsentence.

When she opened the door, Alex was standing there in a ripped T-shirt and cutoff jeans, looking incredibly young and incredibly good and holding her Incredibra.

"Fred dropped this off." He held the bra up like a fishing trophy. "I've only seen this once, but I'm assuming it's yours?"

"Yes." Nina shoved lustful thoughts from her mind and made a grab for it.

"Hold it." Alex moved it away from her. "How do I know it's yours? Put it on and let's see if it fits. I'll check. It's okay because I'm a doc—"

"Give me that or you'll *need* a doctor," Nina told him under her breath.

"Nina?" Michael said from the living room.

"A date?" Alex raised his eyebrows.

"Unfortunately, yes." Nina held out her hand. "Give me my bra."

"Unfortunately?" Alex grinned at her. "Can't get rid of him, huh?"

"I've tried everything but he won't take the hint." Nina glanced back over her shoulder to make sure Michael hadn't come to join them. "If you'll just give me my bra, I'll go—"

"Let me handle this." Alex walked past her into the living room. "Hi, I'm Alex." He held out his right hand, but Michael's eyes were on the bra in his left. "This?" Alex waved it at him. "Nina left it in my apartment last night. Here you go, honey."

Nina grabbed the bra and rolled it up so it didn't look quite so bright and lacy. "Thank you, Alex. You can g—"

"Nina and I are big film buffs." Alex strolled toward the TV. "Great classic on tonight. I'm sure she told you we needed to see this, but you're welcome to stay and watch, too." He punched the button on the remote and flipped through the channels while Michael looked accusingly at Nina and Nina glared at Alex.

"He's a film student," Nina told Michael. "I'm helping him with his coursework so he can graduate and get a real job instead of being a deadbeat like he is now."

"That's my girl," Alex said over his shoulder. "Ah, here we go." He sat down on the floor with his back to the couch and watched the screen where two small children with springs on their heads were talking to Santa.

"What classic is that?" Michael asked suspiciously.

"Santa Claus Goes To Mars," Alex said. "My professor says it's a perfect example of existential angst."

"Really." Michael was still suspicious, but now he was also confused.

"Of course, it's an adaptation of that great Russian novel by Turgid." Alex smiled up at Michael. "You know Turgid?"

"I think I read him in college," Michael said. "Depressing, right?"

"Hell, yes." Alex nodded at the screen where adults with springs on their heads had joined the children. "This is the commercial version. Americans." He shook his head in disgust.

"Right," Michael said, and Nina took pity on him.

"Well, Alex needs to study now, so why don't we call it a night?" She slipped her arm through his.

He pressed closer to her, and she lost any sympathy she had for him and pulled him toward the door.

"When can I see you again?" Michael asked.

Fred growled at him, and Alex shot Michael a look from the floor that was surprisingly vicious. "We're going to be working pretty hard on this film stuff until I graduate," he told Michael. "Better not call her until after then."

Michael looked back at him coldly. "And when will that be?"

"At the rate I'm going?" Alex beamed at him. "I should be out by June of '99."

Michael rolled his eyes and let Nina lead him to the door. "You know, I'd be jealous if he wasn't so much younger than you," he told Nina. "Nice of you to help the kid out."

"Yeah," Nina said, turning her head so his kiss fell on her cheek. "I'm the motherly type."

When Michael was safely on the other side of the door, she went over to Alex and kicked him on the shin.

"Ouch!" He rubbed his leg. "Be careful, woman. You could seriously injure somebody doing that."

"No problem," Nina said. "You're a doctor. You can fix it. And if you can't, you'll always have your *film school degree* to fall back on."

Alex turned back to the TV. "Where did you find that weenie?"

Nina ignored him. "Did you really think he'd believe somebody made a movie called *Santa Claus Goes To Mars?* How dumb—"

The picture on the TV changed to two robots and a voice-over said, "We'll return to *Santa Claus Goes To Mars* after these messages."

"I told you. It's a classic." Alex patted the floor next to him. "Come here, sweetheart, and learn what real film-making is. But first, get the Oreos."

"I don't believe this," Nina said, but she got the Oreos anyway and sat on the couch behind him, giggling over "Mystery Science Theater" and Fred's futile attempts to

schmooze Oreos, and marveling over all the humor and warmth in her life now that Fred and Alex were part of it. The only thing her life needed now was great sex, but she was pretty sure that wasn't part of Alex's equation, regardless of all the careless flirting he did. Why else would he keep showing up with videos and no moves? He wanted a friendship. Fine. That was what she wanted, too.

She looked down at the curve of his shoulder, pressed against the couch near her, and thought wistfully how nice it would be to lean down and kiss him on the neck, just to feel her lips against his skin, just to let him know she was there.

"This is the good part," Alex said over his shoulder, and she smiled at him and said, "This movie has nothing but good parts," and dragged her attention back to the screen where it belonged.

"HOW'S IT GOING with whatshername? The woman upstairs?" Max asked Alex a week later when they were both stretched out in the doctors' lounge in broken-down easy chairs, their feet on the scarred coffee table.

"Hey, I'm dating other women besides Nina," Alex said, trying to sound worldly and unpathetic. "Lots of women." Then he ruined it by adding, "Not that I'm dating Nina."

"If you're not dating her," Max asked, "how are you seeing her?"

"We watch movies," Alex said. "And it's a damn good thing there are a hell of a lot of them in the world or I'd be out in the cold. Even I'm getting tired of them, but that and jogging are the only reasons I can think of to be with her." He closed his eyes, remembering. "She stretches out on the couch behind me, and I can smell her perfume, and she laughs in my ear, and I swear to God, one of these days I'm

going to jump her, and then she'll never speak to me again."

"Don't be a wuss," Max said. "Do it."

"No," Alex said. "I'm not going to screw this up. I want more than a one-night stand here. I want a multiple-night stand. And besides, I'm considering a plan. If it works out, not even Nina will think I'm a kid."

Max snorted. "This should be good."

Alex thought of Nina again. "God, I hope so."

NINA AND FRED CAME running up the stairs two weeks later on a Saturday afternoon late in June, ready for their after-walk ration of one Oreo apiece, to find Charity sitting on the floor by their door.

"It's almost done, Neen." Charity scrambled to her feet and yanked her blue vinyl miniskirt down with one hand while she clutched manuscript pages in the other. "Only one more chapter to go. I've been working on it night and day, even at the shop."

She hesitated, and Nina realized that she was nervous. She'd never seen Charity nervous before. "It's going to be great," she told Charity, moving toward her.

Fred, already there, wiped his nose on Charity's black stockings as a show of support.

Charity looked down in distaste. "Don't they make antihistamines for dogs? His snot problem is getting worse."

Nina took the manuscript from her. "It truly is going to be great. I've read the first chapters, and they're terrific. Really interesting."

"I don't know." Charity clasped her hands together tightly. "I just don't know. After a while, the chapters all started to sound alike."

Nina sighed in relief. She'd noticed that problem, too. "Well, it'll help in the rewrite if you make Jane learn something each time," Nina told her. "This is a first draft. You'll get it in the rewrite."

Charity looked at her. "You'd be tougher on a writer you didn't know, wouldn't you?"

Nina looked back at her, exasperated. "I am *never* tough during a first draft. You want me to beat you up, fine. But let's get the whole book done first. Then we can look at it and see where it needs fixing. I'll call you all the names you want then."

Charity shook her head. "I wish I knew somebody else to give this to. Another reader, you know? Somebody who doesn't know me like you do. You'd like it just because I wrote it."

Nina flipped through the manuscript, stopping at the ninth chapter title. "Oedipus Rat?"

Charity nodded. "That was Bob. He cheated on me with his mother. Told me he was too busy to see me and then took her to bingo. I thought it was A Sign."

Nina nodded with her. "Yes, I'd think that, too." She flipped through the pages again. "Did I miss something? Where's the chapter on your marriage?"

"It's in there," Charity said. "Keep looking. Chapter ten. It was tough to write."

Nina winced, feeling guilty because she was making Charity relive her one-year disaster. "I'm sorry."

"Yeah," Charity said. "The theme of that chapter is never marry a doctor because they're never home, and when they do come home they're too tired to have sex, so they watch television and go to sleep. This chapter alone is going to be worth the price of the book in heartache avoided."

Nina thought of Alex the night before, propped up against her couch, cheering while Harrison Ford found the ark of the covenant. "You're exaggerating."

"Oh, yeah?" Charity leaned against the door. "One night, in order to jump start my marriage, I met Kenneth at the door in the nude. He kissed my cheek, walked into the bedroom, crawled into bed and fell asleep. It's all in there. Chapter ten—The Naked and The Dead."

Nina started to laugh and then stopped herself. "Okay, you want some criticism? I don't know about these chapter titles. We may have to rewrite some." She tucked the manuscript under her arm and fished her door key out of her sweats' pocket. "And even though I do think this is great, you're going to have to make it a little more up-beat," she told Charity as she put her key in the lock. "We can take care of it in the rewrite, but some of this comes close to being bitter."

"That's because I am bitter," Charity said. "You really think it's too bitter?" She shook her head. "We need another reader on this. Somebody who doesn't know me at all."

Great, Charity wanted other readers. Now she was going to have to go door to door to find somebody for a second opinion. Nina started to shove her own door open and then stopped, remembering a door worth knocking on. "Wait a minute. How about if I get you several other readers?"

Charity looked cautious. "Who?"

Nina pulled her door closed. "Come on. You have to meet Norma." She started for the stairs, and Fred and Charity followed her up to the fourth-floor apartment.

"Norma, this is Charity," Nina said when Norma opened the door, and then she stopped while elegant Norma—dressed in olive cashmere and khaki linen—and

over-the-top Charity—dressed in electric blue vinyl and silver lycra—sized each other up, came to their separate conclusions and smiled at each other. "Charity's written a book," Nina went on when it seemed safe. "Does your readers' group ever read unpublished manuscripts?"

"Well, we haven't before," Norma said. "That doesn't mean we can't start." She opened her door wider. "Come on in and tell me about it," she said, and Fred trotted in.

Fifteen minutes later, they were down the stairs again, and Charity had a new deadline.

"I can finish the last chapter by Thursday," she told Nina. "This is so great of Norma to do this. Can you get the copies run off if I get it to you by Thursday night?"

"Sure." Nina put her key in the door. "Norma can give them out on Friday and then the *next* Friday—" Her voice broke off as she opened the door and heard her television.

"We're out of Oreos," Alex called from the floor in front of the TV, and Fred went to join him.

Charity raised an eyebrow at Nina.

Nina lifted her chin. "I must have left the window open." She led Charity over to the couch. "This is Alex. Alex, this is Charity."

Alex turned from the TV. "Ah, the great author—" he began, only to stop as his eyes traveled up Charity's endless black-stockinged legs to her vinyl miniskirt and lycra tank top.

Seeing Charity for the first time was always an experience, Nina reminded herself. But seeing Charity from floor level would be mind-boggling. It wasn't Alex's fault that his chin was on his knees.

"I've heard a lot about you," Charity said, and Alex climbed to his feet.

"I haven't heard nearly enough about you," he said, and Nina wanted to kill them both.

"I'll go get the Oreos," she said to get away from them, and Alex turned back to her and said, "I told you, we're out."

"I moved them," Nina told him. "I was trying to make a space for the Crock-Pot because you keep bitching at me about it, and I moved them. And then there still wasn't enough space for the pot, anyway, but I forgot to move them back."

Alex shook his head at her. "Don't move things around on me. Stability is the foundation of any good relationship. One day it's moving the Oreos, and the next day it'll be the couch, and then where will we be?" He leaned closer to smile into her eyes. "We've got a good thing going here, babe. Don't screw up."

Nina's heart lurched sideways, but she did her best not to smile back. "I'll get the Oreos. You amuse Charity."

She headed for the kitchen, trying not to stomp, and then jumped when Charity spoke from behind her as she reached for the cupboard door.

"That man was flirting with you," Charity said, absolutely delighted.

"That man flirts with tree stumps," Nina said, absolutely disgusted. "You'll see. Go on back in there and sit down next to him."

"I don't want to see." Charity plopped herself down into a chair. "I'm through with men forever. Every time I see one, I want to spit." She grew thoughtful. "Except for Alex. He seems like a good one."

Nina dropped the Oreos on the table. "Then go for it."

Charity scowled at her. "You're not listening. I'm through with men. You're not. I think you should go after Alex."

"Don't be ridiculous," Nina said, feeling immensely relieved and immensely annoyed that she was feeling re-

lieved. It didn't mean anything that Charity wasn't interested in Alex.

"I'm not being ridiculous." Charity picked up an Oreo. "I think you should seduce him."

"Seduce who?" Alex said behind her.

Charity dropped her cookie. "Don't sneak up on me like that."

"Sorry." Alex crossed to the fridge, shoved the Crock-Pot back, opened the door and took out the milk. "Who is Nina seducing? I may be against this."

"I have a new date," Nina said, mentally kicking herself because now she'd have to dig up somebody to date. Digging up made her think of Charity's idea about digging up James Dean, and she grinned in spite of herself.

Alex leaned on the counter next to her and scowled at her. "Stop smiling. You do not have my permission to seduce this guy."

Nina raised her eyebrows at him. "I don't need your permission."

"Yeah, you do." Alex reached behind her and got a mug out of the cupboard. "You're a mother. You have standards to uphold."

Charity frowned at him. "She's not a mother."

"Yes, she is." Alex nodded at Fred, who was sitting at their feet, giving them his best I-Need-An-Oreo-Desperately look. "Fred's at that difficult age."

Charity looked down at him. "Would that be the Age of Snot?"

Alex snorted. "Come on, Fred. They're being irrational, and *Frasier* reruns are on. Let's go watch Eddie." He picked up the Oreos, and Fred surged to his feet and trotted after him into the living room.

Charity looked at Nina. "That man is nuts about you."

Nina sagged against the counter. "Don't be ridiculous. You can't be ridiculous because I'm being ridiculous enough for both of us. I'm the one who made up a phantom date."

"Why don't you go out with *him?*" Charity said, jerking her head toward the living room, exasperated.

Nina folded her arms. "Well, for one thing he hasn't asked me."

Charity rolled her eyes. "It's the nineties. You're allowed to do the asking now."

Nina snorted. "Ask out a guy who's ten years younger than I am? Right. No."

Charity looked back over her shoulder toward the living room. "You're nuts. He's perfect for you, and you're going to let ten years—"

"That's a lot of years, Char," Nina said. "And Alex isn't perfect for me. You know, he's not exactly mature for his age. His idea of intellectual entertainment is 'Mystery Science Theatre.' He has no serious thoughts."

Charity bit into an Oreo. "Sounds wonderful to me."

Nina sighed. "Well, actually, it's wonderful for me, too, for right now, but what happens if we do end up together and the lust part wears off and I'm stuck with an infant significant other?" Nina bit her lip. "Not that we'd ever end up together. We're too mismatched. I'm *visibly* older than he is, and it's only going to get worse. And there's my body." She stopped and swallowed. "Everything's lower and chunkier than it used to be. You should see the women he dates. They're young and beautiful and—" she made a face "—taut and perky, the whole *Playboy* bit. And you want me to flash him a body that has twenty more years on it than the ones he's used to? There's a limit to how long I can hold in my stomach."

Charity opened her mouth, but Nina overrode her. "And he's at the age where he's probably thinking about settling down. I'm at the age where I'm *tired* of settling down. I don't want to do the big-house bit again. I love this apartment. I love my life." She thought for a moment of her life, which included her big empty bed, a bed that grew bigger and emptier with every moment she spent with Alex. *No.* "We're fine as friends," she told Charity. "In fact, we're phenomenal as friends. But for the rest of our lives? When he's my age, I'll be fifty. Men still look great at forty, but I'll be fifty. I'll look old."

Charity frowned at her in disgust. "No, you won't. You're making assumptions based on the way things used to be. Things have changed. People don't get old at fifty anymore. Hell, the best-looking woman I've seen lately is Norma, and she has to be in her sixties."

"Seventy-five," Nina corrected her.

Charity spread her hands out. "Well, *see.* It's attitude that counts, not age. And I have to tell you, your attitude sucks. You might as well be eighty now, the way you're giving up on life."

"I'm not giving up on life," Nina said, stung. "I'm just not going to make a fool of myself over a younger man."

Charity pushed herself away from the table and stood up. "Nina, take it from me because I know this from experience. No matter what guy you end up with, you're going to make a fool of yourself. You might as well make a fool of yourself over somebody who's worth it. And Alex is worth it."

Nina closed her eyes and thought of Alex out there in her living room, his T-shirt torn and probably on backward, feeding illegal Oreos to her dog, definitely the most desirable man she'd ever known in her life.

"Get me a date fast," she told Charity. "Fix me up with somebody my own age before I do something stupid."

"Doing something stupid would be the smartest thing you could do," Charity said. "But I'll get you somebody. You dummy."

A WEEK LATER, a little past eleven, Nina sat in her window and waited for Fred to return from watering the Dumpster. Fifteen minutes before, she'd given a good-night kiss to Charity's fix-up date, a terrific man named Phillip, and now she sat kicking herself for being so unenthusiastic about Phillip's kiss, when he was so nice and so right for her. If she was going to trash perfectly nice men simply because they weren't Alex, she was never going to find any-- body to date. She pondered her dilemma until it dawned on her that Fred hadn't come back in his usual ten minutes.

Before she could go out the window after him, the phone rang.

"Your dog's down here," Alex said when she answered. "Come on down and get him."

"Just put him out on the fire escape," Nina said, confused. "He'll come up on his own. You know—"

"What's wrong?" Alex said, his voice tense with concern. "Stop crying, Nina."

"I'm not crying—"

"I'll be right up," Alex said. "Don't do anything foolish. I'll be right there."

Then all she heard was the dial tone.

Alex wanted out of his apartment for some reason. It could only mean one thing: another date from hell. Nina tried hard not to be glad Alex was crashing and burning again. Where did he find these women? Suppressing a smile, she went to splash water in her eyes just in case tonight's Antichrist came with him.

She did.

"Poor baby." Alex came through the door, looking overdressed and adult in his navy suit, followed by Fred, looking bored and morose, as usual, and Alex's date.

Nina held a tissue to her eyes and checked out the date.

She was a tall brunette, dressed in formfitting black, absolutely lovely and absolutely furious.

"Oh, Alex," Nina said, and then he put his arms around her and pressed her head to his chest. There she was, too close to that chest again, and now that her cheek was pressed against it, she knew it was as warm and solid as it looked. She lost her place in the program for a moment until Alex said pointedly, "Stop crying, honey." Then she tried a sob, and he held her tighter.

"You're terrible at this," he whispered in her ear.

"It wasn't my idea to cry, you big ingrate," she hissed back at him, not really angry as long as his arms were around her.

"Is this going to take long?" his date asked from the doorway. Fred's nose was dangerously close to her leg, and she was glaring at him and Alex with equal disgust.

"Deirdre, I can't leave her," Alex said. Nina sobbed again and Alex patted her. "Let me get you a cab," he said to Deirdre.

"I'll get my own," Deirdre said and shot Nina a look of pure venom before she disappeared down the stairs.

Alex let go of Nina to close the door after Deirdre. "Good," he said to the door. "You have more money than I do, anyway."

"What did she do?" Nina said, tossing the Kleenex away. "Offer to have your baby on the first date?"

Alex wandered into the kitchen. "You got any beer?"

"No." Nina followed him. "She was very lovely."

"Yeah, she's pretty."

Nina felt depressed.

Alex got two glasses from the cupboard. "She's sharp, too. It was hell trying to coax Fred in through the window so I could call you without tipping her off. I thought I was never going to get rid of her."

So he'd used Fred to get rid of his date. Nina cheered up.

Alex shoved back the Crock-Pot and opéned the refrigerator door to peer into the fridge. "You know, as often as I'm up here, you'd think you'd stock beer for me." He pulled out a bottle of wine. "Wine?"

Nina sat down at the table. "Yes. Thank you. What did she do?"

Alex took two glasses down from the stemware rack and put them in front of her. "We're at dinner, right?"

"Right."

He eased the cork out of the bottle and poured the wine. There was enough for two glasses. "What happened to the rest of this? You hitting the sauce with Fred?"

"No, I hit the sauce with my date," Nina said. "What happened at dinner?"

Alex handed her a glass. "Michael again? I thought we got rid of him."

Nina stuck her chin out. "No. Phillip."

Alex frowned. "Who's Phillip?"

"He's a friend of Charity's. You don't know him. What happened at dinner?"

He shook his head at her. "I don't think you should be dating all these strange guys. At least let me check them out first. Who's Phillip?"

Nina fixed her eyes on him. "What. Happened. At. Dinner."

Alex sighed and leaned against the counter. "We're right in the middle of the entrée. Things are going pretty good

although there's something about Deirdre that's a little..." He sipped his wine as he considered.

"Yes?"

"Intimidating." Alex took another sip of wine. "I like strong women, but Deirdre..." He shook his head.

Nina took her wine over to the table and sat down. "What happened in the middle of the entrée?"

Alex left the counter and sat down, too. "She smiled at me across the table, and said, 'I just want you to know where you stand.' Then she opened her purse and handed me two condoms."

"Oh." Nina blinked. "Well, that's very up front of her. And the condoms are good. Safe sex."

"I know about safe sex," Alex said. "I'm a doctor. And I have my own condoms, thank you, in my wallet and in the drawer by my bed. Any guy who doesn't these days is either stupid or suicidal."

Nina tried not to think about his bed. "Well, she was just being prepared."

"Prepared?" Alex looked at her as if she were demented. "I wasn't even sure I wanted to yet, and she's handing me condoms. Don't you think that's a little presumptuous?"

Nina frowned at him. "So what are you saying here? You're mad at her because you're not That Kind of Guy?" She snorted. "Of course you're That Kind of Guy."

"And two," Alex went on, ignoring her. "Two, for crissakes. Talk about pressure."

"Oh, right." Nina nodded wisely over her wine. "You are over thirty. I suppose the equipment is going soft."

"The equipment is fine, thank you," Alex said, glaring at her. "But there is such a thing as performance anxiety."

"You know, I've learned more about men in a couple of months with you than I did in fifteen years with Guy," Nina said. "I thought men just dived in whenever they got the chance. I would have assumed that you'd take that as a compliment."

"You would have assumed wrong," Alex said. "From now on, I'm staying home and watching television." He perked up. "Which reminds me." He took his wine and got up to walk into the living room. "It's time for film school."

"Too bad I don't have a date to get rid of," Nina said, following him again.

"Yeah." Alex turned on the television and flipped through the channels. "Why didn't you call me about Phillip?"

"Because Phillip was a gentleman and kissed me at the door."

Alex froze for a second and then turned to scowl. "You kissed him on the first date?"

Nina looked at him, nonplussed. "Alex, I'm forty. I don't need your permission to *sleep* with a guy on the first date, let alone kiss one."

"The hell you don't." Alex pointed his finger at her. "You're not used to this dating stuff. You let me check these guys out, and then I'll tell you if you can sleep with them or not." He turned back to the TV and punched the remote again, and a moan from the television caught his attention. He settled down on the floor, his back against the couch. "Ah, yes. This is a classic."

Nina looked at the TV. It was full of writhing bodies on sand. "Exactly what classic is this?"

"This would be *Beach Bunnies From Hell.*"

Nina blinked. "You're kidding, right?"

Alex remained glued to the screen where a man and a woman were either mud wrestling or having impossible sex. "Nope."

Nina stared at the woman on the screen with contempt. Her breasts were high, perfect and unmoving no matter what position she twisted herself into, and she twisted herself into a lot of positions, all of which pointed her breasts like bazookas at the camera. Actually, her breasts didn't look like bazookas; they looked like gelatin molds, quivering slightly but solid clear through.

"You know, breasts like that make a man believe in God," Alex said.

Nina flopped down on the couch, disgusted with him and the movie and more convinced than ever that she would never take off her clothes in front of Alex. "God did not make those breasts. Du Pont made those breasts."

Alex sighed. "I know that. I just want to believe. It's like Santa Claus."

Nina's contempt deepened. "Yes, Alexander, there is a Santa Claus. But those breasts are not real."

"I'd rather believe in the breasts."

Nina picked up a magazine from the side table and thwapped him upside the head with it.

"Hey!" Alex turned around, scowling at her.

Nina scowled back. "Well, you deserve it. You'd rather have breasts that look like gelatin molds than real-life breasts?"

"I'll take any breasts." Alex turned back to the TV. "Gelatin molds, huh? You may have a point."

"Of course I have a point," Nina said. "I bet they don't feel natural, either."

"They don't," Alex said, "but they don't feel bad."

"And how do you know—never mind." Nina held up her hand before he could speak. "I know. You're a doctor."

"Well, no, I found that out dating." Alex picked up the remote. "This is probably not a good movie for us. There must be other classics on tonight that we won't fight over."

Nina watched the channels flash before her eyes and debated grabbing the remote and smacking him with it. She had no idea why she was so violent lately. Fortunately, it was always in connection with Alex who deserved beating, anyway.

"Here," he said. "Now this is a *real* classic."

Nina squinted at the screen. Rosalind Russell was marching completely dressed through a room full of typewriters, blood in her eye. Nina could relate. Then Rosalind went through a door and there was Cary Grant. "This is much better," she told Alex. "What is this?"

"His Girl Friday," Alex told her. "You've never seen this? I can't believe it. You're going to love this. Everything Rosalind has is her original equipment and she doesn't take anything off."

Why would she love that? It sounded boring. He must think she was boring. Nina looked back to the screen and watched Rosalind play verbal Ping-Pong with Cary Grant, their dialogue so rapid she was caught up in it within seconds.

By the time Cary had insisted on meeting Ralph Bellamy, who was dumb enough to think he was going to be married to Rosalind by the end of the movie, Nina was stretched out on the couch, watching raptly over Alex's shoulder, as usual. "This is a very sexy movie," she said once in his ear, and he turned his head to grin at her over his shoulder, his mouth close enough that if she leaned forward a couple of inches, her mouth would be on his.

"I know," he said, and she looked into his eyes for a moment and felt dizzy again, felt the heat rise and cloud her mind and make her body tense. She closed her eyes and tried to think of anything else but Alex and how near he was and how much she wanted him.

Then he turned back to the movie, and she tried to think cool thoughts while Roz and Cary made passionate verbal love on the television screen.

She'd never been happier and more miserable in her life.

5

"DO YOU EVER THINK about just dating one woman?" Alex asked Max the next night over his coffee table and their beers. "Move in with her? Commit?"

Max choked and spit out his beer. "God, no. Don't say terrible things like that to me while I'm drinking." He mopped at the beer on his black shirt. "Oh, hell, and this was a good shirt, too."

"I was just thinking it would be nice," Alex said. "You know, knowing you were coming home every night to the same woman. Comfortable."

Max stopped mopping and squinted at him. "It can't be Tricia the weeper, and Debbie's long gone, and even you're not dumb enough to move in with Deirdre." He shuddered at the thought.

"Dated Deirdre, did you?"

"Only once," Max said. "You wouldn't believe what she did to me at dinner."

"Sure I would," Alex said.

"You, too, huh?" Max shook his head. "I believe in safe sex, but not in the middle of the appetizer. Our waiter almost had heart failure."

"Hell," Alex said, "*I* almost had heart failure."

"So if it's not Deirdre, who is it?"

"Nina," Alex said.

Max raised his eyebrows. "Still Nina? You hadn't said anything for a while, so I thought you'd given up on her."

Alex shook his head. "Nope. Nina is not the kind of woman it is possible to give up on."

Max took another drink. "You've been holding out on me. I didn't even know you'd started dating her."

"I haven't." Alex leaned forward and picked up his second beer. "I'm afraid to ask her out."

Max frowned at him. "I'm just playing devil's advocate here, but if you're afraid to ask her to commit for dinner, how in the hell are you ever going to ask her to move in with you?"

Alex leaned his head back against the couch. "I'm not. At least, not right now. She'd spit on me." He stared miserably at the ceiling. "She was married to Guy Adams."

Max whistled. "Big bucks."

Alex nodded. "Dad's got an opening in the cardiac unit."

Max stopped with his beer halfway to his mouth. "You told me you liked the ER."

Alex closed his eyes so he wouldn't have to meet Max's. "I do. But as you keep pointing out, cardiology is more money. And as Dad keeps pointing out, it's a real career."

"So's the ER," Max said.

"I know." Alex felt miserable. "I know. But I'm thinking about cardiology anyway."

"Yeah, but you're thinking about it as a way to get the money to get Nina." Max shook his head and took a drink. "Bad idea," he said when he'd swallowed. "Never plan a career around a woman."

"You're probably right," Alex said, and then the doorbell rang.

When he answered it, Charity was standing there, all wild red hair and impossibly long legs in a hot pink dress so short he thought for a minute it was a T-shirt.

"I came to ask a favor," she said, and Alex thought of all the men in the world who would love to be in his shoes, and of how much he'd love it if it was Nina in front of him in hot pink asking him for something. Anything. Preferably something that required him touching her. Lying down and touching her. Lying down naked and touching her.

"Alex?" Charity said, and he said, "Sure. Come on in."

She stepped inside the living room, and Max stood up, looking poleaxed as his eyes made the trip from her ankle-strapped heels and thigh-high black stockings to her tangled red hair tied on top of her head with what Alex thought might be another black stocking.

"This is my brother, Max," Alex said.

Max held out his hand and beamed at her. "*More* than happy to meet you."

Charity scowled at him. "I'm a lesbian."

Max pulled his hand back. "Did I *ask*?"

Alex stepped between them. "Can I get you something to drink?" he asked Charity. "Some milk? An Oreo?"

"No." Charity lost her scowl. "Listen, Norma's reading group is going to read my book next Friday." She opened her black vinyl bag, a purse large enough to stock a small country, and pulled out a thick stack of papers held together with a rubber band. "And I thought that maybe you'd read it, too, and come to the group next Friday and give us a guy's opinion of it." She smiled up at him, anxious, coaxing, and Alex thought again what a waste it was for her to be smiling at him. "Nina's coming, too," she told him, and he took the manuscript and said, "I'll be there."

Charity's smile widened. "Thank you. I appreciate it. Truly." Her smile dimmed to about five watts as she looked over his shoulder at Max. "Nice meeting you."

Max nodded. "Give my regards to the rest of the girls."

Charity closed her eyes.

"He's kidding," Alex said. "Knock it off, Max."

Charity ignored Max to turn to Alex. "I'll see you Friday then. And thank you!"

When she was gone, Alex glared at his brother. "Did you have to say that?"

Max shrugged and went back to his chair. "She started it. Boy, that is one scary woman."

Alex followed him. "She's Nina's best friend. If I become a cardiologist, we can double-date."

Max picked up his last beer. "Not in this lifetime. Remember Deirdre? Well, that one would hand you *four* condoms." He shuddered. "What's wrong with women these days?"

"You should know," Alex said, stretching out in his chair. "You're the gynecologist."

NINA GREW more nervous for Charity as the next Friday drew closer, but when she and Charity got to Norma's, the reading group turned out to be small: Norma; Rich; Mary Theresa, a lovely young editor; Walter, a weedy plumber; Steve, a burly accountant; and Alex; all sitting relaxed on Norma's bentwood chairs in Norma's airy living room, sipping Norma's mint lemonade.

"I thought you didn't come to these," Nina whispered to him when she'd joined him after he'd patted the chair beside him.

"Charity asked me," he whispered back, and she thought, *And when did you talk to Charity?* and then shoved the thought out of her mind because it was unwor-

thy and because she had more important things to think about. Like whether Charity would make it through the evening without cutting her throat.

"I told Norma not to tell them I'm the writer," she'd told Nina before they'd walked up the stairs. "I want to hear it all, no matter how bad."

"Good," Nina said, and prayed it wouldn't be bad.

It wasn't good.

First of all, they assumed it was fiction. "Much too episodic," Steve said. Steve looked a lot like a construction worker, bulky and tanned, but Norma had introduced him as "the best damn accountant in Riverbend," so Nina mentally thwapped herself for making assumptions. "Every chapter is a story on its own," Steve went on. "There's no continuity. It makes it hard to follow the story. It's a funny story, but it's easy to put the book down between chapters."

"She needs a through line," Mary Theresa agreed. "A spine to hold the story together until the end. But it's funny, really funny, so maybe the humor will carry it."

"Nope." Walter the plumber looked like an accountant. "It's funny, but it's kind of mean funny. I felt sorry for some of these guys."

Great, Nina thought. This didn't bode well for Charity. Or for Howard Press, for that matter.

"I didn't feel sorry for them," Mary Theresa said. "I've *dated* guys like these."

"No, you haven't." Rich stretched out his legs and sipped his lemonade. "No guy is all bad. Maybe these guys had limits, but they were human beings, too."

So it was a gender thing. Nina thought fast. Women would understand it, but men would feel defensive. Most book buyers were female, but that didn't mean Charity

could afford to offend men. She was going to have to do some rethinking on her male characterization.

Rich was still talking. "I think the author sacrificed character for humor. You know, like she didn't have to make them real as long as they were funny. So they all have one thing that she focuses on and makes fun of. Like they're too anal retentive. Or they're too preoccupied with sex." He looked at Nina and smiled. "Or they're too young."

Nina's face burned, and Rich went on. "So she never sees the real man. She obsesses on this one character trait, and she never sees anything else."

Very funny, Rich. Nina stole a sideways look to see if Alex had noticed, but he seemed to be concentrating on what Rick was saying about Charity's book. Thank God.

And what Rich was saying was important. Charity was going to have to rethink her approach.

Nina, however, was *not* going to rethink hers about younger men.

Rich went on, dissecting Charity's male characters, and Nina watched Charity, prepared to carry her out the door if she looked as if she was going to scream.

Charity sat on the edge of her chair, frowning as she concentrated. "But won't it ruin the story if the men are nice?" she asked Rich. "Won't that make it boring?"

"No." Rich leaned forward. "Because then there will be some suspense. The way this is written now, you know each chapter is going to end in disaster. But if they're nice guys with flaws—"

"Okay, that's a problem I saw," Steve broke in. "Each chapter is a disaster bit. It gets depressing because, you know, you *like* Jane when you read about her. She's funny and she's sexy. You *want* her to be happy. And she keeps dating Godzilla. Over and over and over."

"Right," Mary Theresa said. "It's like, why is she so *dumb?* I wanted her to be smart. She's so funny and she's so smart about other things, why is she so dumb about these guys? There should be something about them that's attractive so you understand why she's going out with them. She's so *blind.*"

"You're right," Alex said, and Mary Theresa smiled at him. Well, that was good, Nina thought. Mary Theresa was very pretty and a lot closer to his age. *See, Rich? He's not interested in me, anyway.*

Alex was still talking to Mary Theresa. "You do expect Jane to learn something after each date. You want her to do better every time."

"Yeah, I wanted her to win in the end," Steve said. "I wanted her to get her act together and end up with some guy, a good guy. I got tired of reading about losers, and then it ends and she's alone and you know she's going to hook up with another loser. So, what's the point?"

Nina couldn't look at Charity. Steve had pretty much just summed up the overwhelming problem of the book, right there. More than that, he'd summed up the problem of Charity's entire life.

Nina leaned forward to get Steve's attention. "How about if she learns something from every relationship so at the end she's ready to start again, and you know she'll succeed this time, even though there's not a happily-ever-after chapter? Would that do it?"

"No," Mary Theresa said. "I like the idea of her learning something and things getting better, but I want to see her make it. That's the payoff. If I've suffered with her through all those dates, and I've got to tell you, you really do suffer through those dates, then I ought to get the payoff, too. I want to see her win."

Norma stirred. "You're all right, I think," she said, looking directly at Charity, "but what bothered me the most was that Jane didn't seem emotionally involved with any of them. It seemed as though she went through all the relationships knowing they were going to fail, so she prepared herself by making wisecracks and making conditions for herself. If she lost ten pounds, the relationship would work. If she wore the right clothes, the relationship would work. She never believed any of the men could love her for herself, no matter what she looked like or what she said." Norma looked at Nina. "Or how old she was. She didn't believe in unconditional love."

Nina closed her eyes and vowed never to come back to Norma's again. At least not with Alex beside her. She didn't dare look at him. He was probably embarrassed. She sure as hell was.

Mary Theresa said, "Did I miss a chapter about a younger guy?" and Nina wanted to groan, but Charity nodded at Norma, caught up in the conversation.

"You're right," she said. "You're absolutely right. I'll fix it in the rewrite."

"Did you write this?" Mary Theresa asked her, incredulous.

Charity flushed and sat back. "Yeah. Sorry it was such a waste of your time."

Mary Theresa beamed at her. "But it *wasn't*. It was funny. And sexy. We didn't talk about that, but the sex scenes were terrific."

"Yeah, they were," Steve said, looking at Charity with new eyes. "Really good."

"I think it's going to be an excellent book," Norma told her. "Once you rewrite it to get some of the kinks out of it—"

"No, leave the kinks," Steve said.

"—it's going to be a terrific novel."

"Do you think so?" Charity said.

"I do," Walter said. "Do we get to see the rewrite?"

Charity's face lit up, and Nina relaxed, more relieved than she'd realized that Charity was okay with the criticism. "You'd read it again?" Charity asked them. "You really would?"

"You bet," Alex said. "It's good stuff."

"I think we *deserve* to see it again," Rich said. "We want to see what happens."

Nina smiled at him and thought, *Thank you, Rich, I forgive you for the age crack.*

Charity nodded, beaming on them all. "Yes. Thank you, yes, I'd love to have you read the rewrite."

"THAT WAS NOT A HELP," Alex told Norma and Rich when Charity had dragged Nina out the door to talk about revisions, and everyone else had left. "Beating Nina up in public is not going to make her want to go out with me."

Norma patted his shoulder. "She just needs to wake up. You'll see. She just needs to be nudged a little."

Alex tried to look quelling. "I'd rather do my own nudging, Norma."

"Well, yes, but you're not," Rich said as he put the last chair back against the wall. "You're just standing there with your finger up your nose waiting for a miracle." He shook his head. "You've got to make your own miracles with women, boy."

Great. Now he was getting his technique with women critiqued. He tried to look unwounded. "Thank you, Rich. I'll try to remember that. As a matter of fact, I'm working on the problem."

"You've been working on it for three months," Rich said. "It only took me half an hour to ask Norma out." He

grinned at the woman he loved. "And two weeks to spend the night."

Norma raised an eyebrow. "That was my decision, not yours," she told him before she turned back to Alex. "And it'll be Nina's decision, too. We were just pointing out to her tonight how blind she's being in not making that decision."

"Well, don't do it again," Alex said. "You keep it up, she won't even watch movies with me."

Rich rolled his eyes and took the tray of glasses out to the kitchen.

"He has a point," Norma said, and Alex gave up and went downstairs to his own apartment where nobody did postmortems on his seduction technique, no matter how much it needed them.

CHARITY CALLED Sunday afternoon while Nina was cleaning the kitchen after lunch and trying not to think about Alex.

"That was something Friday night," Charity said.

"Listen, Char, don't get discouraged." Nina cradled the phone on her shoulder so she could put the milk back in the fridge with her free hand. "I looked at the book again last night, and it's not going to take that much to fix it."

"I know," Charity said. "I'm not discouraged. But I've been thinking. And I think Norma's right, about both of us."

"Us?" Nina echoed, butter in hand.

"Us," Charity said, and Nina sighed and slid the butter in the fridge before she shut the door. "We don't believe in unconditional love," Charity went on. "I keep thinking I have to be sexy and funny and sweet, and then I get mad because I'm never myself, and I figure out some flaw in the guys I'm with and use that to get out so I can be myself for

a while. And then I get lonely and go out and play that dumb game again.''

''Wait a minute.'' Nina stopped with a bowl of macaroni and cheese in her hands. ''That's not true. Look at some of these guys, the ones who cheated or who had mother complexes or—''

''I know,'' Charity said. ''I know some of them deserved to be left. But some of them didn't. Like Alex.''

Nina shoved the mac and cheese bowl in the fridge and slammed the door. ''How did Alex get into your book?''

''The only thing wrong with Alex is that he's ten years younger than you are,'' Charity said. ''That's a stupid reason not to love him, Neen.''

''There are a lot of other things wrong with Alex,'' Nina said. ''He's immature and unfocused and—''

''You're making up excuses,'' Charity said. ''The real problem is that you don't believe Alex could love you because your body is forty years old and your face has some wrinkles. Norma hit it right. You don't believe in unconditional love.''

Nina swallowed. ''It's not that easy.''

''Just because you don't believe in yourself doesn't mean that Alex doesn't believe in you,'' Charity said. ''And you won't even give him a chance.''

''He doesn't want a chance,'' Nina said. ''He—''

''Trust me,'' Charity said. ''I've seen the two of you together. He wants a chance.''

''Charity, you're being romantic,'' Nina said. ''This is real life.''

''Real life doesn't have to suck,'' Charity said. ''And that's how I'm going to rewrite this book. I feel good about the book, Neen. I'm *excited* about this. And I believe things will work out for us if we just believe in ourselves.''

"Good." Nina closed her eyes and wished she believed that, too. "I'm glad, Char. I can't wait to read the rewrite."

"That's what I'm working on now," Charity said. "I just wanted to let you know that I was okay. And that I think you should give Alex a chance."

"Goodbye, Charity," Nina said, and Charity sighed and hung up.

Give Alex a chance. Alex had had plenty of chances and he hadn't taken them. All right, she hadn't been exactly welcoming, but he'd had his chances.

He just hadn't wanted them.

Nina got a glass out of the cupboard and jerked the refrigerator door open to get some ice. The door stuck, and she jerked again, annoyed and frustrated over more than the door, and then it opened at the same time the Crock-Pot fell off the top of the fridge and onto the glass in her hand, breaking it neatly into four jagged pieces before it crashed onto the floor, the glass lid smashing in a million pieces at her feet.

Nina stared at her hand, nonplussed, still holding the largest bottom piece of the glass. Her hand hurt, but there were no marks on it. How had she managed to drop a Crock-Pot on a glass and not cut herself? She shut the door and moved slowly to the counter, crunching glass underfoot, to put the rest of the glass down. She swept the glass up one-handed, moving it into a corner and dropping a towel over it so that Fred couldn't wander into it accidentally. Then she flexed her hand, and a thin red line appeared, running down the side of her thumb and into her palm.

She'd cut herself, after all. It couldn't be too bad, though; it was barely bleeding. Just that thin red line. Even as she had the thought, blood began to seep from under the

cut, and she realized that it wasn't a cut as much as a slice, and that it was deep, and that there was going to be a lot more blood. She moved to the sink as her palm turned red and watched in stunned disbelief as the blood began to ooze from her hand, slow, but steadier than she believed possible.

Blotting it with a towel didn't help. Pressure made it bleed faster. There weren't enough Band-Aids in the world to help this cut. Still too stunned to think, Nina looked in the sink and saw red splashed everywhere. She was going to have to get help.

She grabbed a clean blue-checked dish towel and wrapped it around her aching hand. "You stay here," she said to Fred, and grabbed her keys and headed downstairs to see Alex.

She knocked twice, but there was no answer, and she realized he was on duty. At the hospital. Two blocks away. The towel was stained red now, and her hand ached harder, and she pressed it into her stomach, hoping the pressure would slow the bleeding until she figured out what to do. Call 911 and say what? "I cut my hand?" Not for 911. That was for emergencies. Heart attacks. Car accidents. All she had was a cut on her hand. The hospital was only two blocks away.

Pulling her scattered thoughts together, Nina headed for the stairs.

Later, Nina couldn't remember much of the walk except the ache and the throbbing and the dizziness mixed in with how pretty Riverbend was in the twilight. If she had to bleed to death, at least it would be on a nice evening. But once she was at Riverbend General's ER, elbowing her way in the door, trying not to get blood on everything she touched, the calm evening turned into a madhouse filled with more people than she'd ever seen in her life, all talk-

ing at once. She found her way to the admitting desk and leaned against the counter, keeping her hand low and tight to her stomach so she didn't get blood on anything, hoping the pressure would ease the sharp ache that was turning into pain, a little overwhelmed and a lot woozy and very close to throwing up.

"I cut myself," she told the weedy little desk clerk when he asked what she needed. She meant to show him her hand, but she would have had to raise it above the counter to do that, and it seemed like a bad idea.

"Do you have insurance?" he asked.

Nina blinked. "I don't even have my purse." She bit her lip. "I know a doctor here. Alex Moore. He can vouch for me."

The desk clerk sniffed. "We'll see. Wait here. I'll get a nurse." He marched off, and a minute later a little dark nurse came down the hall and stopped to stare at Nina's stomach.

"What happened?" she asked, gently pulling Nina's throbbing hand away from her T-shirt.

"I cut my hand," Nina said.

"Not your stomach?" the nurse said, still supporting Nina's hand, and Nina looked down and saw that her T-shirt was soaked with blood.

"No," she said. "Just my hand."

"Don't move," the nurse said, and grabbed a wheelchair. "Sit."

"I can walk," Nina protested. "I just need a few stitches."

"Humor me," the nurse said, and Nina collapsed into the chair, suddenly grateful.

Her head was swimming a little, and her hand hurt, and when the nurse unwrapped the towel, it hurt more.

"It'll be okay," the nurse told her. "It's deep and it hurts, but you'll be fine."

"Oh, good," Nina said, and sat dazed while the nurse helped her put her bloody hand in a bowl of disinfectant and pulled out a tray with evil-looking things on it. Nina wanted to say, "Is this going to hurt more?" but she didn't have the energy and she didn't want to seem like a wimp. It was bad enough she'd cut herself in such a dumb way. Alex had told her over and over—

Then she heard his voice in the hall. The desk clerk said, "Some woman was asking for you. Zandy has her in two," and Alex's lazy voice said, "All the women ask for me, Andrew. When will you learn?" He came through the door, somehow taller and broader in his doctor's greens, and said, "What have we got, Zan?" and then he saw her and stopped and said, *"Nina!"*

"I'm okay," she said, but he was beside her, his hand on her stomach, gently peeling up her T-shirt while she tried to tug it down. "It's not my stomach, it's my hand," she told him. "I just bled all over myself."

He stopped and swallowed and said, "Nice job, dummy," and the nurse looked at him oddly, which was the way she'd been looking at him ever since he'd said, *"Nina!"*

He turned to the nurse and said, "Let me see it, Zan," and she stepped back while Alex took Nina's hand from the disinfectant. He sighed and said, "Very nice job," and sat down, pulling the tray closer to him. "Flex your fingers for me," he told her, and she did, wincing. "I know, it hurts. Can you make a fist?" She did, and he put his hand against her fingers, and she was comforted by the warmth there. Then he told her to push against his hand, and it hurt again, but she did it anyway because this Alex, this new Alex, wasn't someone anyone would say no to.

"You're all right," he told her. "No nerve injury. We can put you back together here."

Nina nodded, tired from the pain. "Oh. Good."

Alex touched her cheek. "It's almost over. Hang in there." Then Zandy handed him a syringe full of something and Nina closed her eyes. "It's going to sting like hell, babe," she heard him say, and then her hand stung with the needle prick just the way he'd said, and a few moments later, the pain eased away.

She opened her eyes, and Alex said, "You don't want to watch this," so she closed them again, and tried to ignore the tugging sensation on her hand that she was pretty sure was thread being pulled through her skin. Instead, she concentrated on the pressure of Alex's fingers on her hand and the sound of his voice and the warmth of his body close to hers.

"How'd you do it?" he asked her while he tugged at her hand.

Nina winced, knowing she was going to hear "I told you so." Well, she deserved it. "The Crock-Pot fell on a glass I was holding."

Alex let his breath out. "That's my fault."

Nina's eyes flew open. "How is that your fault?"

He kept his eyes on her hand. "I knew that damn thing was going to fall, and I didn't move it."

Nina rolled her eyes, exasperated. "I could have moved it, too, you know."

"Yeah, but you're dumb," Alex said, and she leaned forward to glare at him and caught sight of what he was doing.

What he was doing was pulling the edges of the wound back together, quietly, efficiently, almost without paying attention, she thought, until she looked up at him and re-

alized he was intent even while he teased her. He knew exactly what he was doing.

"You're good at this," she said, and the surprise was in her voice.

He put the last suture in and sat back. "Don't sound so amazed. I have a med-school diploma and everything."

"I'm sorry," Nina said hastily. "I didn't mean that the way it sounded."

He turned to her and looked down at her T-shirt and closed his eyes for a moment. "You look like you've been in a knife fight," he told her. "Get rid of that, will you? Zan will give you a scrub shirt."

"Sure," Zandy said, looking surprised again.

Alex stood up. "I can't stand looking at that. You scared the hell out of me, woman. Next time you show up here, break a leg or something. The sight of all that blood on you makes me want to throw up."

"I thought doctors weren't supposed to get sick at the sight of blood," Nina said.

"That depends on whose blood they're seeing," Alex said. He opened his mouth to say more, but then there was commotion in the hall, and he and Zandy went to look, and then he was gone.

"I'll be back," Zandy told her. "Don't move out of that chair. You could still be woozy from the blood loss."

"I'm fine," Nina said, but Zandy was already gone, so Nina stood up and moved to the doorway to see what was wrong.

The girl on the gurney that an orderly was shoving down the hall made Nina look like a piker in the spilt-blood department. She was sobbing, and there were people all around her, but all Nina could see was Alex, striding along beside her, giving orders that sounded like Greek in a voice that carried without shouting, calm, focused, completely in

control while people scattered to do what he'd said. The whole time, he smiled down at the injured girl, interspersing comfort with command. "You're going to be all right," he told her as the gurney went past Nina's doorway. "We've got you now. I know you're scared, but you're going to be all right."

By the time the gurney was out of Nina's sight, the girl had stopped crying, and Nina felt like starting.

She went back and sat down, trying not to cry, close to it anyway because he'd been so wonderful, first to her and then to that girl, feeling stupid because all she'd ever seen him as was a good time and a body to fantasize about. She'd been as bad as Tricia. Norma was right; she'd been blind. She might be too old for Alex, but Alex was definitely not too young for her.

Zandy came back in a few minutes later.

"Is that girl going to be all right?" Nina asked her.

"Sure." Zandy picked up Nina's hand and began to swab the bloodstains off. "She's on her way to surgery now, and they'll put her back together."

Nina swallowed. "Alex is good, isn't he?"

Zandy stopped swabbing. "He's the best. Are you okay?"

Nina nodded. "I'm a little rocky. It's been a rough night."

"I brought you a shirt." Zandy handed her a green bundle. "Alex was right about that. You'll be back to normal as soon as that T-shirt is history."

Nina looked down at the gore that covered her shirt. "Right," she said, but she knew she'd never be back to normal again.

Norma would be so pleased.

6

"I JUST WANT to take care of her for the rest of my life, and she won't even consider it," Alex told Max the next night as they sat in Alex's apartment after work. "I walked into that examining room and saw all that blood and almost lost my mind just because it was her, and that's when I knew it was all over." He looked at Max, trying not to be pathetic. "This is it. This is the one. I'm crazy about her, but as far as she's concerned, I'm a kid." He took the beer Max handed him and collapsed back onto the couch, naked except for his shorts, trying to cool off from the heat of the July evening and the heat that just thinking about Nina generated in him. The second kind was the worst.

Max sat across from him, pulled another can from the six-pack he'd just dropped on the coffee table between them and popped it open. "As far as *I'm* concerned, you're a kid. Take those shorts, for instance."

Alex looked down at his Daffy Duck shorts. "There's nothing wrong with these shorts. As a matter of fact, your mother gave me these shorts."

Max snorted. "Oh, that's good. You're wearing Mommy's Daffy Duck shorts. You are a kid, Alex. Face it."

Alex looked at him balefully. "You are not being helpful."

"Sorry." Max chugged some beer and closed his eyes as it went down. He finished swallowing and sighed with

pleasure. "God, that's good. Okay, let me think. You can't ask her out on a date because you're too much of a wuss."

"Thank you, Max."

"So we'll have to cut to the chase. Have you tried just asking her to sleep with you?"

"No," Alex said, "because she would say no. I have to get some moves here because just asking isn't going to do it."

"Well." Max shifted in his chair. "This isn't my way, of course, but have you tried hinting?"

"It's not my way, either," Alex said, "but hell yes, I've tried hinting. If I hint any more, I'm going to be one of those guys who goes 'heh, heh, heh,' after every sentence. It's not working, and she's driving me *crazy*."

Max pushed the six-pack closer to Alex. "Have a drink."

"I have one." Alex stopped thinking about Nina for a minute to concentrate on his brother. "Max, you're drinking too much."

"No, I'm not," Max said and finished his beer.

"I'm not kidding." Alex sat up. "For the past couple of months, every time I've seen you, you've had a six-pack in your hand. That's not good, especially considering our genetic makeup." He stared at the can in his own hand for a moment and then put the can on the table, still half-full. "In fact, considering Dad's little problem, neither one of us should be drinking."

Max picked up his second beer. "I've got it under control."

"Max—"

Max held up his hand. "I'm not kidding. I never drink before work. I never drink in public. I never drink alone. And a couple times a week I buy a six-pack and come over here and relax where I know there won't be any more booze once I'm finished with my three, and there won't be any

hassles, and I can forget all the crap and just shoot the bull with you.''

Alex stopped, dumbfounded. ''This is it? This is the only time you drink?''

Max sighed. ''Hell, Alex, have you seen me drinking any other time lately?''

Alex thought about it. ''No. Not since Christmas, anyway. All what crap?''

Max waved the thought away. ''Nothing. I just like coming over here and kicking back. Is it a problem?''

''Hell, no.'' Alex leaned back into the couch again. ''I'm always glad to see you. Sorry. About the booze lecture, I mean.''

''Don't be.'' Max closed his eyes. ''Believe me, I know how easy it could be. I've been watching Dad for thirty-six years, remember? I wish to hell somebody had bitched at him before things got out of control.'' He opened his eyes and grinned at Alex, and Alex felt a rush of love for his brother that was completely out of character.

''I had a bad day a couple of months ago,'' Max went on. ''One of many lately, and I got a six-pack on the way home and stood in the kitchen and drank the first two, and then I thought, 'Christ, two beers, standing up, alone?' '' Max shook his head. ''I poured the other four down the sink, and it was a lot harder than I thought it would be. That's when I decided that unless I was with you, I wasn't drinking. You never screw up, so I knew as long as I was with you, I'd be fine. I swear, this is it. You're my control.''

''Anytime,'' Alex said, touched by his big brother's faith in him. ''Hey, anytime.''

''Well, don't go mushy on me,'' Max said. ''Now let me give you some advice about Nina.''

Nina. Alex groaned and fell back against the couch again. ''There is no advice. I have known that woman for

three months. If she was at all interested, she'd have said so by now."

"No, she wouldn't have," Max said. "She's ten years older than you are."

Alex glared at him. "That doesn't—"

"Not to you, it doesn't matter," Max said. "It does to her. Women do not handle turning forty well."

Alex looked at him with contempt. "And you know this because of your vast experience in dating hundreds of women twice."

"No," Max said, sounding not at all perturbed. "I know this because I'm a gynecologist."

"Oh," Alex said. "Right."

"Forty is when they start rethinking plastic surgery," Max said. "They look at magazines and see all those damn seventeen-year-old anorexics in push-up bras, or they go to the movies and see actresses with tummy tucks and enough silicone to start a new valley, and then they look at their own perfectly good bodies and decide their sex lives are over."

Alex thought of the gelatin-mold conversation he'd had with Nina a couple of weeks back and winced. "Oh, *hell*."

"And if you tell them their bodies are normal and attractive, they think you're being nice," Max finished. "Sometimes, I swear to God, I'd like to set fire to the fashion industry. They're screwing with my women's heads."

Alex raised an eyebrow. "Your women?"

Max looked philosophical. "I like to think of all women as my women. I'm just here looking out for them."

Alex nodded. "The way you couldn't look out for your mom when Dad dumped her."

Max pointed his last beer at Alex. "Don't try to be Freudian. It's not only useless, it's out-of-date. Think Jung."

"I don't want to think young. That's the reason Nina won't look at me now."

Max looked at him with disgust. "And you wonder why I drink when I'm around you." He finished his beer and put the can on the table. "I haven't met Nina, so I'm sort of working in the dark here, but my guess is that if she's spending that much time with you, she's interested."

"We're friends." Alex picked up his beer again, needing the alcohol. "She likes me."

"Well, that's a hell of a good start, Alex," Max told him. "What you have to do next is kiss her."

The thought of first Nina's mouth, soft and pink, lips parted, and then of his mouth on Nina's mouth, hot and hard, was such a jolt to Alex's system that he shivered.

"Boy, you've got it bad," Max said.

"I can't kiss her," Alex said, recovering. "She'd slap me silly and never let me back in her apartment."

Max shook his head. "Nope. You just have to pick your moment. Sooner or later, if she's interested at all, she'll give you an opening. It may be just a little one, just the way she holds her head when she looks at you, or a hesitation at the door, but she'll give you one." He picked up his last beer and leaned back. "And then, my boy, you take it and run with it."

Alex thought about Nina and the way she always looked over his shoulder when they watched movies. Sometimes he'd turn his head and her mouth would be so close, he'd almost go for it until he'd think of the look that would be in her eyes if he tried it: startled, insulted, upset. Nope. "I'll lose her. One wrong move and I'm history up there."

"Wait for it," Max said. "There'll be a moment, trust me." He took another drink. "There's only one real problem."

Alex closed his eyes. "Only one? I see about twelve."

"When you finally get your shot," Max said, "don't blow it. You'd better be the best damn kisser in North America, or she's going to remember the ten-year difference and say no."

"Thank you, Max." Alex drained his beer and cracked another one. "I'm going to drink these next two beers and throw up now."

"You can do it," Max said. "Hell, *I* did it under a lot worse circumstances."

"Did what?" Alex sat back with the rest of his beer. "Kissed North America?"

"No, seduced an older woman." Max smiled, remembering. "Betty Jean Persky."

Alex swallowed more of his beer, trying to remember Betty Jean Persky. "I have no recollection of this woman."

"She was a senior, I was a freshman," Max said. "They said it couldn't be done."

Alex frowned. "You're talking about college? Hell, Max—"

"I'm talking about high school," Max said. "And if you think ten years is a big difference now, you try getting a senior cheerleader to look at you when you're a freshman science geek."

Alex thought about it. "You may have a point."

Max nodded. "That's what I'm telling you. You pick your moment, and then you make damn sure she's never been kissed like that before." He shrugged. "Of course, I was a damn good kisser even at fifteen."

Alex nodded. "I remember you practicing on the dog. So how did you get Betty Whosis to kiss you?"

"Kissing booth at the Spring Boosters Carnival," Max said. "I paid a buck."

Alex grinned at him. "And?"

Max grinned back. "And that was the last time I paid a buck to kiss Betty Jean Persky. Hell of a set of lips, that Betty Jean." He grew reflective. "Helluva summer before she went off to college. She's a prosecuting attorney in Columbus now." He shook his head. "I do remember her fondly."

"I don't think Nina is going to volunteer for a kissing booth," Alex said.

"Well, then, you'll just have to wait until she volunteers for something else," Max said.

UPSTAIRS, a couple of hours later, Nina had her own problems.

"Really, Guy," she told her ex-husband. "I'm fine. It was a bad cut, but the ER stitched it up. I'm perfectly okay."

"Nina, if you were at the emergency room, you weren't perfectly okay." Guy sat relaxed on her couch, tall, dark, handsome, sure of himself and annoying as hell. "I was stunned when they called my office for your insurance number. My wife in the hospital and nobody calls me until the next day?"

"Ex-wife," Nina said automatically. "They shouldn't have called you but they got confused. And I'm fine. See?" She held her bandaged hand up in front of her. "All fixed up and taken care of. Thanks for coming by, but—"

"But you're not taken care of." Guy leaned forward, earnest and patronizing. "You can't take care of yourself, Nina. You never have. You need someone to look after you. That's why I kept up the insurance after the divorce. I knew

you wouldn't think to get any. See, I'm still taking care of you. You need me.''

He looked very smug as he spoke, and Nina repressed the urge to throw something heavy at him. It wasn't his fault he was convinced she couldn't exist without him. She'd spent a good part of their marriage convinced of the same thing. She felt sad for him suddenly, for the boy she'd married so long ago and laughed with so long ago and made love with so long ago, a boy who'd worked night and day until he'd grown up to be a successful suit without a sense of humor. That was one of the many good things about Alex; no matter how successful he became, he'd never lose his ability to laugh.

Poor Guy.

She shook her head at him. "I did get insurance through Howard Press, Guy. I'm covered. I appreciate it, but I'm covered. And I can take care of myself perfectly well. In fact, I have ever since the divorce. I *like* taking care of myself.''

"Yes, I'm sure you do," Guy said, obviously not listening to a word she'd said. "And now that you've proved that to yourself, I think it's time we talked.''

Nina gave up on tact. "We have nothing to talk about, Guy. We're divorced. We're not supposed to talk.''

Guy looked deep into her eyes. "I think we could make it work again, Nina.''

Nina gaped at him. "What?''

"I was wrong, I know that.'' Guy looked honestly guilty and honestly miserable. "I had a midlife crisis, and you got fed up and left, and I understand that I wasn't paying enough attention to you. I nearly ruined everything, I understand that. But I'm over that now, and I think we could make it work this time.'' He leaned closer. "I've changed.''

He reached across the space between then and flicked a curl off her forehead.

Nina jerked back. She'd left him because she was fed up and wanted a new life, and he'd still managed to turn the divorce into something about him. Amazing. She tried not to glare at him. "You can't mean you want us back together."

"Yes." Guy gazed into her eyes. "I didn't realize until I heard that you were hurt how much I've missed you. How much you need me to take care of you. How much I want to take care of you. And I know you've missed me, too, living in this tiny apartment with a *dog,* for heaven's sake." He looked at Fred with contempt.

Fred looked back at him with more contempt.

Guy gave up and turned to Nina and shook his head. "All alone. I don't like to think of you alone."

Nina closed her eyes. He thought she'd go back to him just because he asked. Well, that was Guy for you. He was ready to be married again, so she must be, too. "Look, Guy, I'm happy in this apartment. I like—"

"Living alone?" Guy finished for her. "Sleeping alone?" He smiled at her. "You liked sex too much to be happy sleeping alone now."

Nina pulled back, indignant. "What makes you think I'm sleeping alone?"

Guy shook his head. "I know you, Nina. You're not the type to have casual affairs. And let's face it, it's not easy for women of your age to meet someone new. The numbers are against you. There are more single women than men in their forties, you know."

You smug bastard, she thought, but what she said was, "He's thirty."

Guy blinked. "Who's thirty? You have a thirty-year-old lover? You're joking."

"Why?" Nina scowled at him. "You've dated younger women since we've been divorced. Compared to most of them, Alex is practically senile."

"Alex." Guy leaned back against the couch, his confidence in place again.

"Alex." Nina nodded. "He's a doctor. A resident at Riverbend General."

"This is the kid you told me about, the one who lives downstairs, right?" Guy said. "You're sleeping with your thirty-year-old neighbor." He shook his head again. "Not you, Nina. You're a lovely woman, but you look your age. And you know how people would talk. You'd never do anything that humiliating."

Over by the window, Fred whined and scratched at the screen. "Excuse me," Nina said with exaggerated dignity and went to let him out before she picked up a knife and eviscerated her ex-husband.

Humiliating, she fumed as she unlatched the screen. Well, that was just fine. It was liberating for him to screw around with twenty-somethings, but it would be humiliating for her to make love with—

Unbidden, the thought of making love with Alex leaped into her mind, and she stopped for a moment. It wasn't unfamiliar after three months of dreaming about him, going hot whenever he was near her, all but leaping on him every time he appeared in her doorway, but for the first time it seemed feasible, something she might actually do. Seeing Alex in the ER the night before had jarred her ideas about him considerably. His hands had been so sure as he'd stitched her up, and he'd been so focused, so controlled. She thought of his hands again, and then she thought about them on her, unbuttoning her blouse, unhooking her bra...

And then she thought of her body, softened with age, everything lower than it used to be, lower than Alex was

accustomed to, Alex who dated twenty-somethings with silicone embellishments. Even if he was interested in her, he'd only seen her clothed. She could hide a lot of flaws with clothing. But naked . . .

Guy was right. She looked her age.

"Nina?" Guy called to her, impatient, and she remembered his "humiliating" crack.

So, all right, maybe making love with Alex wasn't something she could do, but Guy didn't need to know that. It would be great if Alex would drop by and flirt with her. Okay, that was juvenile of her, but it would be great. Just long enough to make Guy wonder.

Fred whined again, and on an impulse, Nina grabbed a pen from the table and wrote "Help!" on his collar. "Go see Alex," she whispered into his ear, and then she slid the screen out of the window. "Alex," she whispered again as Fred tensed himself for his leap. "Alex."

Then Fred jumped, and Guy moved off the couch and over to a chair by the window to join her while she waited for Fred to come back.

Twenty minutes later, Guy was presenting another logical reason why they should reconcile, and Nina was getting ready to go down the fire escape to look for Fred the Unreliable. If Fred had been Lassie, Timmy would still be in the well, growing gills.

"I don't know where he got to," she said, peering out the window. "He hasn't done this since the first day I got him."

"Will you forget that damn dog!" Guy scowled at her. "I'm telling you, I think if we saw a counselor, we could—" The pounding on the door stopped him in midsentence, and he turned, his scowl changing to a glare. "What the hell—"

"Nina?" Alex's voice through the door was frantic. "Nina, open up. Fred's collar—"

Nina ran to the door, threw it open and grabbed him before he could say anything else. "Alex! Darling!"

Alex stood in the doorway in Daffy Duck shorts and a white T-shirt that was on backward and inside out with the label sticking out like a flag under his chin. He blinked at her. "Darling?"

"Daffy Duck?" Nina said, looking down.

"Darling?" Alex repeated. "What's going on? Fred's collar—"

"Darling!" Nina said again and threw her arms around him, planting a quick, clumsy kiss on his parted lips to shut him up as she tripped against him. "I was just telling Guy about us."

"About us." Alex's arms had gone around her when she'd thrown herself at him, and he looked down at her now and shook his head. "You told Guy about us. Well, I hope poor old Guy took it well."

Alex's arms felt great around her, but it was hard to think with him pulling her close. What were they talking about? Oh, right, Guy. Guy who was still there. Nina began to turn back to her ex-husband. "Well, actually, he's still—"

"Because I'm not giving this up," Alex finished and kissed her.

Nina froze for a moment when his mouth touched hers and his arms pulled her tight against him. She made a tiny sound and then her brain shorted out, and there was a rushing in her ears, but mostly there was just Alex, everywhere, his body against hers, his mouth on hers, everything about him wiping out reality. He pulled her closer, and she tried not to moan at the ache in her breasts as they squashed against his chest, and then he slipped his tongue into her mouth, and shut down all her thoughts and her knees went away. She grabbed at his shoulders and closed her eyes, and all there was in the world was the lush heat of

his mouth on hers and the glow that pulsed from her solar plexus because he was pressed against her.

"Oh, God," she breathed when he moved his lips off hers, nibbling his way across her cheek to her ear.

"He doesn't look like he believes us," Alex whispered in her ear, and the tickle of his breath made her shudder against him. "I think we're going to have to have sex on the couch to convince him." He began to pull her toward the couch, and Nina was so blasted with lust for him she would have followed him anywhere, but Guy cleared his throat.

"Oh, you're *here*." Alex peered toward the window at Guy. "Sorry. Thought we were alone."

"Nina and I were discussing our reconciliation. Weren't we, Nina?" Guy's voice demanded an answer, but Nina leaned against Alex's chest, clutching him to her, still mindless from his kiss, and said, "What?"

Alex grinned down at her and tightened his arm around her, and she felt the heat flare again and breathed harder. *Stop this,* she told herself and turned her head to look at Guy. Looking at Guy was usually a complete turnoff, so that should help her get her mind back.

Guy was surveying Alex's outfit with palpable scorn. "So this is what an up-and-coming young doctor wears these days, is it?"

"Only on his way to get laid," Alex said cheerfully, and Nina shivered at the thought and he held her tighter. "Nice suit," he said to Guy. "Bet it takes hours to get out of that."

Nina tried to listen, but she didn't give a damn what Guy said. He'd been irrelevant before, but now he was invisible. She had things to think about. Like why Alex had French-kissed her to impress Guy when Guy couldn't have known the difference. Alex must have wanted to. Of course,

he did like women in general. It didn't mean anything in particular.

Don't lose your grip here, Nina told herself, and then Alex moved his hand down her side to her hip, and the heat that small stroke generated in her made her dizzy all over again, and she let her head drop to his shoulder.

"I'll talk to you tomorrow, Nina," she heard Guy say from far away, and she said, "Mmmhmm," not caring, and then the door shut behind him, and she was alone with Alex.

Nina tried hard to pull herself together. "Uh, thank you. That was—"

"Shut up, Nina," Alex said, and kissed her again, and Nina leaned into him so eagerly that she gave up any hope of pretending to herself that she didn't want him.

He had the most amazing mouth. She'd known since yesterday that he had surgeon's fingers, but this was the first she realized he had a surgeon's mouth. He could work miracles with that mouth. He could bring the dead back to life with that mouth. He sure as hell was bringing her back to life with that mouth. She wanted to tell him that, but to do that she'd have to take her lips off his, and she had no intentions of ever taking her lips off his, of losing that insanely glorious stroke of his tongue in her mouth, of...

He was pulling her toward the couch, and then down on the couch with him, and then he rolled to pin her underneath him and the length of his body was hot and hard on hers, and she clutched at him, opening her legs to bring him closer to her as he pressed against her. All the while he kissed her, his tongue teasing her mouth open, his lips on hers, and then on her neck. He shoved her T-shirt up and cupped his hand around her lace-covered bra, and she cried out at how good the pressure felt against her swollen breast. She'd never wanted any man so much, never wanted hands

and mouth so hard on her, never wanted to be taken so roughly before, never wanted to be so marked and possessed. She wrapped her legs around him to bring him as hard against her as possible, and he rocked his hips into hers, biting her shoulder while she gasped and clutched at him, and then his mouth was on hers again, bruising her, and she was lost, tearing at his T-shirt, trying to rip it off. He rose a little to help her, and she pulled it over his head, clutching it in her hand while she arched up to meet him, but he said, *"Nina!"* and his voice was full of horror, not lust.

He jerked away from her, grabbing her wrist and pulling her up into a sitting position, and from far away she focused on her hand and saw blood.

"Oh, hell," Alex said, and she looked at him, broad and beautiful in the lamplight, his chest furred with blond hair and his muscles clenched from holding her up, his mouth dark from kissing her and being kissed, and she thought, *What's a little blood?* and kissed him again.

He kissed her back, hard, and then groaned and said, "Nina, love, we've ripped some stitches, let me look at it," and she moved to his mouth again.

"No," she said. "It's all right. Kiss me now."

And he did, but his kiss was gentle, not hot. "I hate this, but I have to fix your hand, Nina," he whispered to her. "You're hurt. Let me fix it."

He sounded so much like Guy that she woke up. "All right," she said, and used her free hand to pull her T-shirt down while Alex unwrapped the bandage.

"It's not bad," he told her a moment later while she was still coming down from her sexual high. "We can fix it here. Do you have a first-aid kit?"

Nina felt tired suddenly. "In the bathroom," she told him.

Alex kissed her again, still gentle. "Stay here," he told her. "Don't get any ideas about moving."

She watched him cross the floor to the bathroom, naked except for those damn Daffy Duck shorts, and she wondered if she'd lost her mind. If her hand hadn't started to bleed, she'd have been naked with him in another five minutes, and he would have been glorious—he was glorious even in Daffy Duck shorts—and she would have been middle-aged with a middle-aged body.

Good thing her hand had started to bleed.

She met him halfway across the floor, half expecting him to say, "I told you to stay put," but he just bandaged her hand again, standing there in the hallway.

"Are you okay?" he asked her when he was done. "I'm sorry. I never—"

"It's not your fault." She patted him on the shoulder with her good hand, and he looked unhappier than she'd ever seen him. She reached around him and opened the door. "Thank you for helping me with Guy."

Alex stood there for a moment, looking confused and hesitant and sexier than anybody else on the face of the earth. "Nina, could we talk about—"

"No," Nina said, pushing him gently out the door. "I'll see you tomorrow."

"Nina—" he said, and then she closed the door in his face and leaned her forehead against it. Her hand throbbed from the stitches, and her body throbbed from his hands, but mostly her mind throbbed from how much she wanted him and couldn't have him and how close she'd been to disaster.

Fred licked her ankle.

"Thank you, Fred," she told him. "You did good tonight. Just like Lassie, after all."

She went back to the couch to turn off the lamps and saw Alex's T-shirt on the floor. She picked it up and held it to her face, inhaling his scent for a minute while Fred watched. "I've got it bad, Fred," she told him. "I've got it so bad I'm going to sleep in this T-shirt tonight, that's how bad it is."

Fred yawned.

"Yeah?" Nina said. "Wait'll you fall in love. It's the pits."

"YOU WERE RIGHT," Alex said ten minutes later when Max picked up the phone.

"I'm always right," Max said, yawning. "I also have to be at the office tomorrow at eight. Could you tell me about your triumph tomorrow night? I'll bring the beer."

"It wasn't a triumph," Alex said gloomily. "It was close, but then her hand started to bleed, and by the time I had her bandaged again, she said no."

"Never stop to bandage," Max said.

"That's very humanitarian of you, Dr. Moore," Alex said. "And I still don't know why she stopped. I bandaged her hand, and she looked at me and said, 'Thank you and good night.' I still don't know what I did wrong."

He heard Max sigh on the other end of the line. "Let me think for a minute." There was a long silence, and then Max's voice came cautiously. "I hate to ask this, you couldn't have been this dumb, but you did change your clothes before you went up there, didn't you?"

Alex was lost. "My clothes?"

"Hell, Alex, you're hopeless," Max said.

"Since when are you the big clothing authority?" Alex asked, annoyed. "I haven't noticed you dressing like *GQ*."

"Alex, listen to me carefully," Max said. "I'm telling you this as your brother and as your best friend."

"All right," Alex said. "Let's have it."

"Never wear Daffy Duck shorts to seduce a woman. You want her gasping in awe when she looks down, not wondering how old you are."

"Oh, *hell,*" Alex said.

"I'M WORKING on the rewrite," Charity said the next evening when Nina picked up the phone.

"Great." Nina tried to open the window for Fred while she kept the phone clamped between her ear and her shoulder. She wanted to tell Charity everything about Alex and the kiss and the couch, but she didn't want to think about it because she'd been thinking about it all night and all day and she was already half-crazy with lust. Talking dirty about Alex on the phone to Charity would not help things. Much better to discuss the book. "Did you work on a new last chapter, too?"

"Yes." Charity hesitated. "I'm making some big changes, Neen."

Nina stopped moving. "How big?"

She heard Charity draw a deep breath. "I'm making it fiction."

Nina closed her eyes in pain. Fiction. Sexy, romantic fiction. Jessica would have a fit. "Tell me you're kidding."

"No, no, I'm serious. I'm making it fiction." Charity's voice speeded up. "The whole reading group thought it was, anyway, and it's *so* much better, Neen. I just changed all the names, and after I did that, I saw how funny all the stories were. And I'd already made it third person and used my middle name for the heroine, so now all I have to do is write all the chapters over again so they're upbeat and she learns something each time."

"Fiction," Nina repeated, still trying to compute that she'd gone to contract on a book of erotic fiction for Jessica's stuffy Howard Press.

Jessica's father was going to turn cartwheels in his grave. Jessica, on the other hand, would just fire her.

"Yeah, and I'm making the guys better, too. I thought about them, and I'm doing another rewrite now, showing why she falls for them so her mistakes don't seem so dumb." Charity sounded so happy that Nina tried to listen to her and be happy, too. "Which gave me the idea for a great title since it's about mistakes now instead of just bitching. What do you think of *Jane Errs?*"

"*Jane Errs*. That's great," Nina said, still trying to grasp the extent of the disaster.

"And I'm writing the thirteenth chapter now, the happily-ever-after chapter about the perfect man. His name is Raoul."

Nina stared at the phone in disbelief. "Raoul? You don't know any Raouls."

"I've always loved that name," Charity said. "I'm making him a combination of Antonio Banderas, Harrison Ford and Alex."

Nina blinked. "Alex?"

"Yeah, Alex," Charity said. "Alex is a great guy. I still don't understand why you haven't jumped him. I would have long ago."

Nina made her automatic reply. "That's easy for you to say. You don't have a forty-year-old body."

"No, I have a thirty-eight-year-old body," Charity said, her impatience clear even over the phone.

"Charity, parts of me droop," Nina said. "I don't think naked is a possibility here."

"You vastly overestimate how picky guys are about naked women," Charity told her. "A little droop is not going to bother Alex."

"Well, it bothers me," Nina said. "Now, about the book—"

"Then wear the Incredibra," Charity said. "That's about as anti-droop as you can get without surgery. I cannot *believe* that you haven't made a move on that man."

Nina thought about being brave and not discussing her previous night's trauma, and then she remembered it was Charity she was talking to. This is what best friends were for. "Actually, Alex made a move on me. He kissed me last night."

"Great," Charity said. "So how was it?"

Nina slumped against the couch, remembering. "It was phenomenal. I almost had a heart attack when he took off his T-shirt. He has a beautiful body, Char. Really beautiful."

"Wait a minute," Charity said. "How'd we get from a kiss to naked?"

"I don't know." Nina thought about it. "He kissed me, and the next thing I knew, I was under him on the couch ripping at his shirt. I've never been that hot in my entire life."

"Wow. Maybe you'd better rethink seducing him and dumping him. If he's that good, he might be worth keeping around for the long haul."

"Charity, he's a kid—"

"He is *not.*" Charity sounded exasperated. "He's darling and he's fully grown, and he's obviously got all his moves. You have to get over this age stuff."

"Would you date somebody who was twenty-eight?" Nina demanded.

"Probably." Charity's voice was unsure. "It would depend on the twenty-eight-year-old."

"My thirty-year-old was wearing Daffy Duck shorts," Nina said.

"Well, that's unfortunate but not unfixable," Charity said. "Rip them off him."

Nina had a flash of Alex naked. He looked wonderful. "Absolutely not."

"How did he ever manage to get you to kiss him, anyway?" Charity asked. "For that alone, he should get some kind of seduction badge. You're so uptight about this guy, you've practically put up an electric fence."

"I was trying to make Guy jealous."

"That was very mature of you, dear. Did it work?"

"I don't know. He left while I was kissing Alex."

"You want my advice?"

Nina thought of Charity and her twelve chapters of romantic disaster plus one romantic triumph with the fictional Raoul. "No."

"Here's what you do," Charity told her. "You take off all your clothes, and put on your trench coat, and climb down the fire escape and into his window, and when he says, 'Excuse me?' you take off the coat."

"Not in this lifetime."

"Do it," Charity said. "Trust me."

"Right." Nina tried to imagine herself naked in Alex's living room. It was too humiliating to contemplate. "Even if I could do that, I wouldn't know what to do next."

Charity snorted. "You won't have to do anything. He'll take it from there. In fact, from the sounds of things, he'll take it from the minute you climb in the window. Trust me—this is going to be the easiest seduction you've ever done."

"I've never done any seduction at all."

"Well, then it's time to start. Now let me tell you about Raoul."

Nina hung up the phone five minutes later, trying to distract herself with the knowledge that her career was going to be over as soon as Jessica got a good look at *Jane Errs*. It didn't work. All she could think of was Alex, and Alex's body, and his heat, and his hands, and his mouth, and the weight of him against her, on top of her. Making love with Alex. The thought was so overwhelming that her mind shut down and her body took over, swelling with heat as she closed her eyes and imagined him the way he'd been the night before.

She needed him. It wasn't just gee-wouldn't-it-be-nice lust anymore. She wasn't going to be able to eat or sleep or think if she didn't have him soon.

And he wanted her. She was pretty sure that Charity was right: all she'd have to do would be crawl through his window and take off her clothes. Except she couldn't possibly do that. Not possibly.

But, oh, Alex. She closed her eyes and thought of him again, lovely and loose-limbed and broad and strong, and the heat in her thickened and became a clawing in her veins. For months she'd been wanting him, trying not to think about him, thinking about him anyway, and then last night, he'd touched her and made all her fantasies reality. She wrapped her arms around herself, pressing hard, trying to stop the itch, but it was everywhere and the only thing that could save her was touching Alex.

All right then.

She walked into her bedroom, stripped off her clothes and looked at herself naked in the mirror as positively as she could.

Gravity had betrayed her when she wasn't paying attention. Looking closely, she could see the damage. Cellulite. Fat. Bulge. Droop.

She drew a deep breath. Well, okay, so nothing was the way it used to be. But it wasn't bad. And it was all real, no gelatin molds. So she wasn't Cindy Crawford. Big deal. Without the airbrushing, Cindy Crawford probably wasn't Cindy Crawford, either.

Nina crossed her arms over her breasts and closed her eyes. It was irrelevant anyway because if she didn't have Alex, she'd die, and this was the only body she had to take him with. So her choices were either to take her clothes off and let Alex see her naked or never to sleep with him ever. And she had to sleep with him.

Maybe she wouldn't have to take all her clothes off.

"I could wear the Incredibra and keep the lights off," she said to her reflection, and went to paw through her underwear drawer. There at the bottom she found her red lace Incredibra, the one she couldn't return since Fred had dragged it down the fire escape. "This is it," she told Fred, who'd followed her into the bedroom. "I'm really going to wear it this time." She put on the bra and the red lace underpants, cut high enough to at least disguise the fact that her stomach wasn't flat and then squinted at herself in the mirror.

Her breasts had never been this high. Nobody's breasts had ever been this high. Incredibras had so much lift they could get Fred off the ground. Well, that was good. And all that red confused the eye. She could get away with it.

She went into the living room and dug her black trench coat out of the closet. "You stay here," she told Fred while she put it on. Then she took a deep breath and pulled the screen out of the window and went down the fire escape.

Alex's window was open, and she climbed through into his darkened living room, only to freeze when she heard voices in the lit kitchen.

Oh, *great.* He had a date, and she'd just crawled into his living room in her underwear. She turned to escape back through the window and knocked over the floor lamp. *Hell.* She grabbed the lamp and righted it, and then turned to go, but Alex was there in the lit doorway in his T-shirt and pgedduck shorts, looking more desirable than any man she'd ever seen in her life.

"Hello?" he said, and turned on the living-room light, blinking when he saw her.

Nina backed toward the window. "I was just leaving."

"No, you're not," Alex said, and then another Alex, this one black-haired, came out of the kitchen carrying a can of beer. "This is my brother, Max," Alex said, not taking his eyes off her. "He was just leaving."

"No, I wasn't." Max looked at Nina with interest.

Alex glared at him. "This is Nina."

"I was just leaving." Max turned toward the door. "In fact, I'm already gone." He opened the door, looked at Alex and said, "I told you to get rid of those damn shorts," and left.

Alex turned back to Nina. "Hi."

"Hi," Nina said, feeling like a fool.

7

ALEX SEEMED HESITANT. "I'm glad you're here. I thought maybe you weren't talking to me because I'd, uh, kissed you."

Okay, this was it. If she wanted him, this was it. She was going to have to do it.

Nina took off her coat and dropped it on the floor, and stood there with nothing but red lace between her and Alex.

Alex blinked. "On the other hand, talking isn't everything. Is that the Incredibra Fred brought me?"

Nina nodded.

He exhaled slowly and walked toward her. "It's very nice. Take it off."

Nina felt dizzy as he reached for her, and then she went into his arms, wrapping herself around him, almost crying out because he felt so good and she needed him so much. "I need you to make love to me," she said in his ear, and her voice came out thick with lust. "I need you now. I don't care about anything else. I just—"

His mouth closed over hers, and she moaned into him, tasting him with her tongue as his fingers dug into her back and then her rear end, pulling her tight against him even while she arched into him and bit his lip.

"Bedroom," he gasped when they came up for air. "We move now, or I take you on the floor."

Nina let him pull her toward the bedroom, dazed with wanting him, crazy to feel him inside her, but when they were in his room, and he stripped off his shirt and said, "Really nice bra. Take it off," Nina came crashing back to reality.

"No," she said, crossing her arms over her breasts.

"Nina—" he began, moving toward her.

"Turn off the lights." She took a step back until she was up against the bed.

"Sure." He reached back and flipped the light switch and then reached for her again. "Take it off."

"Alex, you don't understand," she said, and he stopped. She swallowed, trying to explain. "Everything's *lower* than it used to be."

"Nina, you don't understand," Alex said. "I don't care if it's on the *floor.* I want you naked now."

"Alex—" But then he was kissing her, hooking his foot around her ankle and tripping her back onto the bed until she fell, bouncing under him as his body moved over hers, his mouth hot on her neck.

"Alex," she tried again, holding on to sanity as his hands made her weak with heat, and then he looked down into her eyes, and she was stunned by the passion she saw there.

"I want you," he said. "I want you and I need you *now.* Do you want me?" He slid his hand down her side and pulled her hips closer to his, and she clenched her teeth as she felt him hard through his shorts.

"Oh, God, yes." Nina moved under him, crazy at his touch. "I can't stand it anymore. *Yes.*"

"Then you're losing the bra." Alex unhooked the center clasp with one hand and pulled the lace away from her body, and before she could wince, his mouth was hot on her throat and then on her breast, sucking hard, and she arched under him, mindless in the blast of pure pleasure his lips

and tongue sent through her, any qualms she had forgotten, any fear gone. She raked her fingers through his hair and moaned as he licked and sucked at her swollen breasts, and then Fred barked at her.

He was sitting beside the bed.

Nina gasped and blinked, pushing halfheartedly at Alex's head while she tried to remember her name.

Alex stopped and looked down at Fred. "Where did you come from?" he asked, and then shook his head. "I don't care. Go back."

"I left the window open," Nina said around ragged breaths as she struggled to sit up. "I'll put him back. I'll—"

"No, you won't." Alex pressed her back down with his body, and she shuddered under him, loving the slide of her breasts against the fur of his chest and the pressure of his body between her legs as he bore down on her. "You're not getting out of this bed," he told her.

"No." Nina ran her hands down his body and watched him close his eyes in pleasure. "No, I'm not. I'm not getting out of this bed." She rocked her hips against his and shuddered at how good he felt. *"Do things to me."*

Alex looked down at her, and his eyes were black with lust. "I intend to do things to you." He looked at Fred. "Pay attention. You may pick up some pointers here."

Nina moved against the pillow. "He's just a child. He shouldn't be watching."

Alex pressed her hips harder into the mattress, letting his hand trail down her shoulder to cup her breast, his thumb teasing her nipple. Nina moaned, and Fred whined, and Alex frowned down at him, his hand still driving Nina into mindlessness. "Think of this as cable TV," she heard him tell Fred. "Not your mom and dad finally having great sex." Then he leaned down and licked her nipple, and Nina

rolled her head to the side, drunk with pleasure, and saw
Fred yawn and lick his lips.

"Go *away,* Fred," she said, but Alex said, "Good idea,"
and began to kiss his way between Nina's breasts and down
the slope of her stomach, tickling her and making her
shudder, sliding the red lace of her underpants down as he
moved his body across her thighs.

"Oh, God, yes," Nina said through clenched teeth, and
then he reached her hips and licked inside her, and Nina lost
all power of speech. Her body went liquid under his hands
and his mouth and all she knew was flooding heat and
pressure and a tightening deep inside her that Alex was
making tighter and tighter. She twisted under him and
arched, and he held her still, his fingers biting into her hips
while he stroked his tongue inside her over and over again,
and the combination of his tongue and his hands and the
knowledge that she was with Alex, finally with Alex, and
that she was going to have all of him pushed her over the
edge, and the heat broke inside her, and the spasms shook
her body, moving her against his mouth as she came and
came. Then he was kissing his way across her stomach,
sucking on her breasts, biting at the hollow of her neck
while she wrapped herself around him and rocked away the
last of her orgasm.

She lay with her head back, trying to breathe, trying to
hold on to the glow, vaguely aware that he was reaching
across her to open the drawer beside the bed, feeling his hip
against hers as he stripped off his shorts, and then hearing
foil tear. Thank God; a condom meant he'd be inside her
soon. She rolled against him and breathed, "Hurry," in his
ear, and he laughed a little, low and lazy, and then pulled
her on top of him.

"That's the last thing I'm going to do," he told her, and
she put her hands on his chest and pushed up enough so

that she could see into his eyes. "This is going to take all night," he promised her. "I'm going to watch you come over and over again. You're going to come seeing the dawn, I swear it."

She shivered, and his hand slid up her neck, and his thumb moved across her lips, and she licked at him and then bit him as he moved underneath her. He eased his hand down her side and between her legs and slid his finger into her, stroking her until she moaned against his chest, and then she felt him move hard against her stomach. She dug her fingernails into his shoulders, crazy with anticipation. He pulled her up to him and she helped, moving against him, wanting him between her thighs, filling the emptiness there, and then he was inside her, hard inside her, and she jerked against him as his fingers pressed into her flesh, pulling her against him. She was slick and hot, and she moaned at the slide and the friction and the pressure and the shudder in her blood as he moved inside her.

"Oh, *Nina,*" he said, and pulled her face back down to his, his mouth on hers, licking into her mouth as he rocked up into her body, and after that, there was nothing for the rest of the night but Alex and Alex's hands and Alex's mouth, and Alex's body over hers, under hers, inside hers, making her mindless with need and speechless with release over and over again.

They stopped once for Oreos—"I've never eaten Oreos naked before," she told him when he brought the package and two mugs of milk back to bed, and he said, "From now on, we eat all our Oreos naked"—and they showered together at three in the morning, almost too exhausted to stand but too crazed with need for each other to stop. Then they fell asleep, wrapped around each other, but a few hours later Alex stirred against her and said, "I've wanted you too long not to have you again," and his hands pulled

her closer, and groggy with sleep and desire she said, "I've wanted you, too, so much." Then she kissed his shoulder and then his nipple, moving down his body this time, feeling his fingers clutch her shoulders and then wind into hair when she found him and took him hard in her mouth, loving the way he moaned when she did and the way he felt, smooth and hard against her tongue. And when he pulled her back up to him, he kissed her roughly, bruising her mouth and making her crazier for him than ever. He made love to her again then, taking her high and hard this time so that her climax crashed over her and left her shuddering and gasping against him as he came, too.

And the last thing Nina saw, while she was still trembling from the aftershocks of her climax, just before she fell asleep with Alex's arms wrapped around her, was his bedroom window turning light with the dawn.

"YOU LOOK LIKE HELL," Max said to Alex when he ran into him at the hospital the next day.

"That's funny, I feel great." Alex yawned and shook his head to stay awake. "I just told Dad I'd take the cardiology spot. I am now the number-one son. Sorry about that."

"Be my guest." Max frowned at him. "I don't get this. You want to be a cardiologist about as much as I do. What the hell are you doing?"

"You want to know the truth?" Alex said. "I'm not sure about cardiology, but I'll be an ax murderer if that's what it takes to keep Nina."

"To keep Nina?" Max raised an eyebrow. "Which means you think you have Nina."

Alex thought of Nina, warm and naked and loving in the dark the night before. "I have Nina," he said soberly. "Now I have to make sure I keep her. She was married to Guy Adams. She's used to money and parties and real

houses, not apartments in chopped-up old Victorians. She's used to real life.''

"Sounds boring," Max said.

"Maybe to us, but not to her." Alex drew a deep breath. "She still thinks I'm a kid, and she's right. I stay in the ER because I like it, not because it's a good career move. I've never given a thought to the future because I thought the future was going to be like yesterday. I've been acting like a kid, living like a kid, and Nina's not going to want to live that way." He thought of Nina again, but this time it was the old Nina, the one who'd treated him like a younger brother, platonic and loving. Last night, he'd demolished the brother problem. Now all he had to do was prove to her that he was mature, that he could keep her safe, the way Guy had. The memory of Guy in Nina's apartment flashed back to him, Guy sneering and saying, "So this is what an up-and-coming young doctor wears these days, is it?" *Back off, buddy,* Alex snarled in his thoughts, but he could see why Nina had married the creep. Big, handsome, rich, successful. He set his jaw. It was time he stopped being up-and-coming and came. That made him think of Nina again. He couldn't lose her. "It's time I got my act together," he told Max. "Started a secure life. Nina deserves it."

"Have you discussed this with her?" Max said. "She may not give a damn about the money."

Alex set his jaw. "I give a damn. She's going to have everything she had before." He clapped Max on the shoulder. "Thanks for the advice, by the way. You were right."

"I'm always right," Max said. "Which advice?" When Alex laughed and began to walk away, Max added, "Well, here's some more. I think you should talk to Nina about this cardiology thing. You know, she *left* the guy with the money the last time."

"I know what I'm doing, Max," Alex said over his shoulder. "She's going to have everything."

"Whether she wants it or not?" Max called after him, and Alex ignored him.

He had enough qualms about what he was doing. He didn't need Max adding more.

"LATE NIGHT?" Jessica said brightly when Nina staggered into the office two hours late.

Nina nodded. "I was, uh, up with a friend."

"Lucky you," Jessica said, and Nina started, not quite sure she'd heard such a non-beige comment from her boss. "How's Charity's book coming along?" Jessica added, and Nina caught an underlying note of tension in her voice.

"She's in rewrite," Nina said. "I should have it edited within a couple of weeks." She swallowed. "I can show it to you then. There are a few things—"

"No." Jessica held up her hand. "You don't need to discuss it with me. I trust you. In fact, I don't even need to read it at all."

Nina gaped at her. Jessica read everything that went out from Howard Press, not because she didn't trust her editors but because she loved the Press and its books. Something was wrong here.

"You did say you thought it was going to be popular, didn't you?" Jessica asked, and this time her intensity was unmistakable.

The wolf must be at the door. And judging from her intense interest, Jessica must be hoping that she could throw Charity's book at it and scare it away.

"I think it's going to be very popular," Nina said.

Jessica nodded. "Well, then. Not that popularity matters, of course."

Nina nodded. "Of course not."

When Jessica had gone back to her office, Nina collapsed into her chair and thought about the situation.

Jessica knew there were going to be things in Charity's book that she wasn't going to like.

Jessica needed a bestseller.

So Jessica was going to ignore the book until it was published, and then tell people, "Well, I hadn't actually seen the book before it went to press so I was *surprised*, of course, but it's doing very well for us, so..."

But Jessica didn't know that the book had turned into fiction. Howard Press didn't print fiction.

Nina thought about the problem from all the angles. What it came down to was that Jessica had stuck her head in the sand, so it was Nina's decision. And Nina's decision was that it was time for Howard Press to print fiction.

She took a deep breath and called Charity. "When can you have that book done?"

"The end of the week," Charity said. "It's going like wildfire now that it's fiction."

"Shhhhhh!" Nina hissed. "Good. Get it to me this weekend. This is going to be the fastest edit any book ever had. We want this out fast."

"Why?"

"Because you're going to save our butts, babe," Nina told her. "Write good."

"I am," Charity said. "What's wrong with you? You sound like you're on speed."

"My life has been very exciting lately," Nina said.

"It'd be a lot more exciting if you'd go downstairs and jump Alex," Charity said.

"I did."

"*What?* Oh, for joy, for joy, for joy!" The phone bumped and Nina pictured Charity doing a modified bunny hop around the boutique, Charity's time-honored method

of showing happiness beyond expression. Charity came back on the line. "This is so great! This is beyond great!" Then her voice grew cautious. "It was great, wasn't it?"

"The earth moved, the stars wept and the sun turned cartwheels 'cross the sky," Nina said. "The greatest sex since time began."

Charity moaned. "Oh, terrific, now I'm jealous."

"He has a brother," Nina suggested. "Looks just like him except with dark hair."

Charity snorted. "Max. Him I've met. No thanks."

"Well, you can't have Alex," Nina said. "He's mine." Then she realized what she'd just said and stopped.

"Oh," Charity said. "Like that, is it?"

"Probably not," Nina said, but when Alex came home that night, it was exactly like that.

"This is not just a two-night stand," he told her sternly when they were lying exhausted on her hall floor, having made love inside her door because they couldn't wait to get to her bedroom. "We have a future."

"A future," Nina echoed, still trying to regroup her senses after orgasm. "Futures are good."

"You, me and Fred," Alex said. "Forever. Except from now on we find something softer to do this on or my knees will be shot."

"Okay," Nina said. "A future, huh?"

"I know what you're thinking." Alex sat up, and Nina watched the muscles in his back flex and thought, *If you knew what I was thinking, you'd be back down here with me.* "You're thinking I'm not responsible enough for you," Alex went on. "That I can't give you the life Guy gave you."

Nina sat up. "I don't want—"

Alex put his hand over her mouth. "I know you'd never say anything about the money, but it's important to me. I want you to have everything."

Nina peeled his hand away. "I have everything."

Alex ignored her. "So I told Dad I'd take the cardiology position."

Nina blinked. "I thought you didn't want it. I thought you wanted the ER. I thought—"

"This is what I want," Alex said, and Nina shut up.

Great. He was going to be a cardiologist. A lifetime of cocktail parties and conventions stretched before her. Fundraising for the cardiac unit. Opening nights. All the garbage she thought she'd escaped when she left Guy. All starting all over again.

And that was the worst part. It was *starting* all over again. She'd helped Guy build a career, and now she got to build another one. If she'd stayed with Guy, at least she wouldn't have had to do this garbage all over again.

Then she looked at Alex and felt terrible. It wasn't his fault she was a retread. If she'd been in her twenties instead of her forties, she'd be champing at the bit to help him out. If this was the price she had to pay for loving Alex, it was worth it. Alex was worth anything.

Even wearing that damn Incredibra for the rest of her life.

"Great," she told him. "This is great."

"Charity, this book is really great," she said two weeks later when she and Charity were sitting on the living-room floor drinking Amaretto milk shakes, celebrating this time. "I had to do practically no editing. It's wonderful. It's tight and it flows and it's funny and the sex scenes are incredible. I read one to Alex last night, and he jumped me."

"You could read the phone book to Alex and he'd jump you," Charity told her.

"Not necessarily," Nina said, and Charity stopped with her milk shake halfway to her mouth.

"Uh-oh," she said. "Trouble in paradise?"

"He's working with his father," Nina said. "Getting ready for this cardiology thing. Long hours. He's a little tired." Actually, he'd fallen asleep in front of the TV before Harrison Ford had found the Holy Grail. She'd tried to be understanding, but it was definitely a bad sign.

Charity nodded. "Kenneth."

Nina closed her eyes and groaned. "Don't say that. I want this to work."

"It will." Charity slurped some of her milk shake. "That's what I found out writing this book. I gave up on him too fast. We might have made it work. I mean, he was a great guy, he was just trying to start a big career."

Nina thought about Alex. "I'm sure you're right." Then she realized what Charity had said. "Are you sorry you divorced Kenneth?"

Charity shook her head. "Nope. That was years ago now. I'm going forward. But I've learned from it. The next guy I hook up with is going to be my last. My Raoul."

Nina's thoughts went back to Alex. "It's not just the sleeping. He's drinking too much."

"Alex? He doesn't seem like the drunk type."

"He's not." Nina bit her lip. "His brother shows up four or five nights a week with a six-pack and they split it. And then they both look at the empty cans the way Fred looks at an empty Oreo wrapper."

Charity scowled. "Well, there's your explanation. It's his brother."

Nina shook her head. "No, it's not. Max is a good guy. In fact, Max is a great guy. The rest of Alex's family is sort of cold, but Max has been great from the start."

"Sort of cold? You didn't tell me you met his family."

"We had dinner." Nina's face twisted as she remembered. "His father looked at me and said, 'We were hoping Alex would have children.'"

Charity winced. "Ouch. What did Alex say?"

"He said, 'No, we weren't,' and Max said, 'Can I get you a drink, Nina?' and Max's mom did something to his dad and he sort of flinched and shut up. But it was ugly. And then there was the dinner with my family."

"Oh, boy. How is your mother? Still flash-frozen?"

"She was very polite to Alex," Nina said. "And then after dessert, she pulled me to one side and said, 'What are you going to do when he leaves you for a younger woman?'"

Charity rolled her eyes and picked up her milk shake to finish it off. "So I guess you and Alex won't be spending the holidays with the families."

Nina laughed shortly. "Just with Max. I like him a lot. We'll make our own family with you and Max and Fred."

"Well, if you're planning on marrying me off, I'll take Fred before I take Max." Charity stood up. "Listen, I've got to go. Thanks for the milk shake."

"Wait a minute." Nina scrambled to her feet. "Don't you want to talk about the book?"

"No. The book is finished. I wrote it and rewrote it and rewrote it and now I want to forget it for a while. Do I need to rewrite it again?"

"No," Nina said. "I'll do the final edit and send it to you to check over, and then we'll send it to the printer. Jessica put a hurry-up on it, so we should have bound ARCs in a month."

Charity stopped stretching. "ARCs?"

"Advance Reader Copies. They go out to reviewers so we can get some good review quotes for the jacket."

Charity's arms dropped to her sides. "Lots of reviewers?"

"For your book, yes." Nina bent to pick up their milk shake glasses. "I'm sending this one to every reviewer on the planet. It's going to be great."

"I hope so." Charity's voice sounded hollow. "I really want this to be good, Neen. I've never done anything with my brains before."

Nina blinked at her. "Of course you have. You run that store beautifully."

Charity swallowed. "I mean creative brains. I already have an idea for another book. I really want this to work."

Nina hugged Charity, wrapping her arms around her so that the glasses in her hands clanked as she clutched her. "It's going to work," she promised her, while she said a silent, fervent prayer that it would, not only for Charity's sake, but for her own and Jessica's, too.

"SO HOW'S IT GOING with Nina?" Max asked Alex at lunch the next week in the hospital cafeteria.

"Nina's great." Alex tried to sound happy but a yawn overwhelmed him. "Life's great."

Max raised an eyebrow at him . "Well, don't let the enthusiasm make you lose your grip."

"No." Alex shook his head and then regretted it. It felt as if his brains were rattling in his skull like mushy marbles. "I mean it. She's great."

Max leaned back. "And how's cardiology?"

Alex tried to focus on him. "Cardiology? Cardiology sucks."

Max shook his head. "Why don't you knock this off and go back to the ER and make everybody happy?"

Alex glared at him. "People are happy I'm in cardiology. Dad's ecstatic."

Max looked at him with disbelief. "How can you tell?"

Alex ignored him. "And Nina's going to be happy once I get this work schedule ironed out. Pretty soon I'll be out of the ER, and then—"

"And then you will be miserable," Max finished. "I can't believe you're doing this to yourself. And for what? Nina will love you no matter what you do. She's great, the best thing that ever happened to you. And you're missing it because you have some dumb idea that she needs to be rich."

"I'll tell you what's a dumb idea," Alex told him. "The Incredibra. That's a dumb idea."

Max nodded. "Yes, I can see how we got from cardiology to bras. Makes perfect sense. A word of advice—get some sleep before you kill a patient."

"I may kill myself first," Alex said, and then blinked. "Forget I said that. I don't know what I'm saying."

"You're saying you're unhappy." Max stood up and shoved his chair back, and the screech it made on the floor made Alex wince. "Stop this, Alex. You're going to end up like Dad. And me."

Alex blinked up at him. "You? What's wrong with you?"

Max looked down at him, and for the first time, Alex saw his brother as an older man, not just a guy to pal around with. "I'm thirty-six, I've poured my whole life into my career, I'm burned-out and I'm alone," Max said, and his voice was like lead. "I'm tired, and I've got nowhere to go. And no one to go to. You have Nina. Hell, if I had Nina, I'd grab her and go to a beach somewhere and just watch

the sun come up and go down forever. You've got it all, and you're throwing it away. Don't screw this up, Alex."

Alex swallowed. "You're exaggerating."

Max nodded, defeated. "Probably. I'll be by with a six-pack tonight, and we can forget I said that together."

"Good," Alex said. "Make it a twelve-pack. I've got some other stuff to forget, too."

"SOME OF THE advance reviews are back, Charity," Nina said to her a month later on the office phone while she stared at the letters before her. "We're just getting them."

"Well, how *are* they?" Charity demanded.

"They're good," Nina said. "They're really good. They're just not what I expected."

"Like what?" Charity said. "Nina, you're *killing* me here!"

"Like 'funniest sex farce in years,'" Nina read to her. She picked up another review. "Like 'Moll Flanders meets Odysseus.' Like '*Jane Errs* will do for boutique owners what *Jane Eyre* did for governesses.' Like 'Read *Jane Errs* and find out all the things your mother never taught you about sex.'"

"That's good, right," Charity said dubiously.

"Well, it's going to sell books," Nina said.

"Didn't they notice the other stuff?" Charity said. "How she changed? What she learned? Didn't they notice the *important* stuff?"

Nina flipped back through the reviews. "They seem to be concentrating on the sex, but that's probably because they weren't expecting it. Howard Press doesn't usually publish a book like yours."

Or as one of the reviews put it: "This book blows a hole in the side of stuffy old Howard Press and lets the light of

the twentieth century in. The surprise is that it's the bedroom light."

Jessica was going to have heart failure when she showed her the reviews.

But what Jessica did instead was fire her.

"It's fiction?" she screeched to Nina when Nina gave her the reviews.

"It started out as a memoir." Nina clasped her hands in front of her. "It truly did, but in the last rewrite, Charity changed it to fiction, and it was better that way, and the reviews are good—"

Jessica waved a review at her, apoplectic with rage. *"Listen* to this review! '*Jane Errs* makes the rest of the Howard Press output look like a bad blind date.' That's what you call a good review?"

Nina gave up. "Well, yes. I call that a good review."

Jessica stopped waving paper around and leaned on her desk. "You're fired."

Nina stepped back. "I'm what?"

"You're fired. You're out. And you take this book with you because I'm not releasing it. Not now, not ever. Howard Press will never print trash."

Nina regrouped. "Okay, fine, fire me, but release Charity's book. It's not trash. You haven't even read it yet, how can you say it's trash? That's intellectually dishonest. For heaven's sake, Jessica, it's already in production. You can't—"

Jessica leveled a look at her that stopped her cold. "I can do anything to save the reputation of my father's press. And I will. Now get out."

THAT NIGHT, Alex tried to comfort her. "It's all right, you don't have to work, anyway. I can support you. That's what

I wanted to do, anyway. It'll be just like when you were married to Guy.''

"That's a great comfort to me," Nina said. "And I'm sure it will be a great comfort to Charity, too."

Then she went to Charity's apartment to tell her in person.

Charity's face went blank with shock as she sank onto her wicker couch. "She's not going to release it? It's printed. Why won't she release it? I'm not going to have a book, after all?"

Nina sat beside her. "Let me think. I'll fix this."

"Why didn't you tell her it was fiction?" Charity asked.

"I thought it was better that she didn't know," Nina said. "She didn't want to know. I thought she'd just have to accept it."

"You thought wrong," Charity said, her voice dead.

Nina jerked her head up. "Listen to me, I'm going to fix this."

Charity shook her head, defeated. "How? It's over."

"The hell it is." Nina stood up. "There are other presses and this is a great book. It even has advance reviews. We'll just buy it back from Jessica and sell it somewhere else."

Charity nodded but her heart wasn't in it. "Sure, Neen. Whatever."

"I'll fix this," Nina said.

"I'M NOT SURE I can fix this," Nina told Max the next night at dinner.

It was his father's birthday and the family had gathered for cake and booze. "It's a Moore tradition," Max had told her, filling her glass. "By the time the candles are lit, so are we." His mother and his sister had toasted his father briefly and coolly and then left the room, and now it was just Nina

and the three Moore men, who were looking more and more alike: tall, good-looking, strained and unhappy.

Max was looking particularly miserable.

"Are you all right?" Nina had asked him, searching his eyes.

"No," Max said. "But thanks for asking." He smiled at her, a small smile but a genuine one. "I hope to hell Alex talks you into marrying him soon. It's about time we got a human being in this family."

"I don't think marriage is a good idea," Nina said.

Max snorted. "Why, because you want to give him an out in case he grows up and changes his mind?"

Nina set her jaw. "It could happen."

Max shook his head. "Not if he has any brains. And notwithstanding his performance lately, he has brains."

"I don't," Nina said. "I just lost my job because I'm stupid."

"Tell daddy," Max had said, and Nina had dumped it all in his lap.

"I'm sorry to bore you with this," she said when she was finished, "but Alex tells me not to worry about it since he'll be supporting me, anyway." She looked across the living room where Alex was discussing something somber and cardiac with his father. "So I told Fred. It was a help, but not like telling you."

"Forget the book," Max said. "Save Alex. Hell, save me."

Nina watched Alex across the room, nodding at something his father said, and he looked so much like his father that she felt cold. "He doesn't laugh anymore. We've been together for almost two months now, and he doesn't laugh anymore. We don't watch movies or jog because he's too tired. Even Fred knows something's wrong. He whines un-

til Alex pays attention to him. It's like he knows Alex has to be reminded to live life."

"Send Fred to my house," Max said. "Do you want another drink?"

"No," Nina said. "I didn't want this first one." She turned to Max. "And neither did you. If you're so unhappy, *do something about it*. Stop anesthetizing it with alcohol."

Max blinked at her anger. "Hey, don't take it out on me because Alex is turning into the old man. I told him not to do it, but he wanted to give you the rich life."

Nina stopped. "What are you talking about? Are you telling me he doesn't want cardiology for himself?"

Max snorted. "Of course not. He loves the ER. He's doing it for you."

Nina gritted her teeth. It was Guy all over again. Doing it for her when she didn't want it. Alex and his father came to join them and she glared at them with such passion that Max patted her hand, but they didn't seem to notice.

"Alex and I have worked out a wedding present for you, my dear," his father said.

The hell you have. Nina smiled tightly. "We're not getting married."

His father smiled back at her, oblivious. "Now, now, Nina, there's no need to feel guilty because you're past childbearing age. As Alex has pointed out, it isn't that important. Max isn't married yet."

Alec winced, and Max looked at her and said, "I'll flip you for the right to say something nasty here."

"So we bought you a house," his father finished, and Nina rose straight out of her chair like a banshee.

"You did what?"

"We bought a house," Alex said, blinking at her. "Dad gave us the down payment. It's on Lehigh Terrace."

Nina gritted her teeth. "I used to live on Lehigh Terrace."

"I know," Alex said. "That's why we bought there. So it'll be just like when you were married to Guy."

Nina gritted her teeth harder, so hard she thought her gums were going to shove through her cheeks. "I *left* Guy. Why are you turning into him?"

His father intervened. "Really, Nina, I hardly think—"

"Yeah, we know," Max said. "That's why you drink. That's why we all drink, so we don't have to think about anything but work and booze. You know, we have a problem here."

His father scowled at him. "What are you talking about?"

Max scowled back. "You're an alcoholic workaholic, and you raised the Drunk Brothers in your own image." He looked at Alex. "Turn back now, boy, or you're going to lose everything."

Alex glared at him. "I don't see why I'm the bad guy because I want Nina to have it all."

"This isn't about me. You don't care about me," Nina said. "If you cared about me, you'd listen to me. All you can hear is your own ego shrieking, 'If I don't give her everything Guy gave her, she'll leave me.'" She grabbed her purse from the table. "I love you, you jerk, but I'm not going to live that damn life again, even for you. I like the apartment, and I like my dog, and I liked my job, and I just screwed up my best friend's life, but I don't have to screw up my own." She shook her head at him, close to tears, so angry she wanted to kill him. "I hope you and your father are very happy in your house and your career. I wouldn't have any of it as a gift, or you, either, for that matter. I was right. You're too young for me. You're so caught up in

your own insecurities that you can't even see me standing in front of you."

Alex put his drink down. "I can see you. And you're wearing that damn Incredibra. You think I don't listen to you? *You* don't listen to me! How about—"

"Good night," Nina said. "I'll find my own way home."

Max stood up, too. "Nah, I'll take you. I'm not going to be popular here, anyway. And since I'm giving up the sauce, I doubt I'll be invited back."

Nina headed for the door, but she heard Max tell his father, "Retire and dry out. It's the only thing that'll save you." When she turned back, he was looking at Alex. "God knows what's going to save you," he told him.

"Wait a minute," Alex said, but Max was heading for the door, taking Nina's arm. "Let's go, kid."

"Will you *wait a minute?*" Alex roared, but Nina walked out into the night, grateful she had Max to lean on, already wishing he was Alex instead.

8

"AND THEN WHAT?" Charity said, the next night over non-Amaretto milk shakes.

"And then I went home and cried myself to sleep," Nina said. "But I did the right thing. I know I did the right thing because I feel so *relieved*. I even spent the day at the library making a list of publishers and planning our book strategy so Alex couldn't find me and convince me to go back to that lousy life he was building for me. I mean, I'm miserable because I love the rat bastard, but I couldn't have gone through another marriage like that one. And Alex was *crazed*. He was bound and determined that I was going to have my old life back whether I wanted it or not. And the only thing he could think to say was that crack about the Incredibra."

Charity frowned. "I don't get that part. Why did he hate the Incredibra?"

Nina closed her eyes and groaned. "Because I wouldn't take it off until the lights were off."

Charity put her milk shake down. "Let me get this straight. You slept with this guy for two months, and you never took your bra off with the lights on? He never saw your breasts?"

Nina frowned back at her. "Don't make it sound so stupid. I'm forty, for God's sake. I—"

"Did he care? Did he say, 'I hate your forty-year-old breasts, wear a bra to bed'?"

Nina glared at her, shocked. "Of course not. He'd never say anything like that. Alex was *wonderful*. He'd tell me how beautiful I looked, and ask me to take it off but—"

"But you didn't listen to him," Charity finished. "You cared more about your own ego than what he wanted. You were just like him."

Nina straightened. "Don't even try to compare us. He bought a damn *house*, and all I—"

"All you did was refuse to let your lover see you naked because you didn't trust him to love you no matter what you looked like," Charity finished. "You don't believe in unconditional love. Neither does Alex. So you both threw away the best thing you ever had because you didn't believe in each other or yourselves."

Nina tried to think of something to say, some way to tell Charity how wrong she was, but it was hard because she sounded so right. Then someone knocked on the door, and her heart lurched, and she thought *Alex,* and scrambled to her feet to let him in.

It was Jessica.

Nina blinked at her on the doorstep. "You're kidding me."

"No," Jessica said. "I've been trying to call you all day. Where have you been?"

Nina gaped at her.

"Never mind. May I come in?"

Nina jerked to her senses. "Oh. Right. Sure."

She stepped back and Jessica walked past her and saw Charity sitting on the floor, feeding a pretzel to Fred. "Hello, Charity," she said. "I read your book last night."

Charity looked wary. "Did you like it?"

Jessica nodded. "Yes."

Charity gaped in unison with Nina this time. "You did?"

"Yes." Jessica looked around for a nearby chair and, not finding one, sat gracefully on the floor next to Charity. "What is that you're drinking?"

"Chocolate milk shakes," Charity said. "We used to put Amaretto in them, but we've seen what alcohol can do so we're not doing that anymore."

"Good for you," Jessica said. "I need you to keep your mind clear so we can talk about your book." She looked at Nina. "You were right. After you left, I thought about what you said, about my being intellectually dishonest by refusing Charity's book without reading it. I read it, and it's wonderful."

"But Howard Press doesn't publish fiction," Nina said.

"It does now," Jessica said. "Times have changed. We're going to change with them. You're hired again."

Nina swallowed. "Oh. Good. I'll get more ice cream."

When Jessica had her own milk shake and they were all seated on the floor, Fred included, Nina said, "So does this mean you'll publish the book, after all?"

Jessica nodded, her mouth full of chocolate and ice cream. "Yes," she said when she'd swallowed, "but we're not going to use those stupid reviews. They missed the point of the book. They missed Jane's *growth.*"

Charity sighed with happiness. "I love you, Jessica. Have a pretzel." Fred moaned, so she fed him another one, too.

"That book is Kierkegaard," Jessica continued. "Pure Kierkegaard."

Charity blinked. "Who?"

"Søren Kierkegaard," Jessica told her. "A Danish philosopher. He said, 'Life must be understood backward, but it must be lived forward.'"

"I like that," Charity said. "'Understood backward and lived forward.' Is he single?"

Jessica blinked, and Nina said, "She's kidding. She has a mouth problem."

"Good," Jessica said. "She'll be wonderful on a book tour."

"A book tour?" Charity echoed, and as Nina sat back and watched, Charity and Jessica bonded over chocolate milk shakes and a belief that her book was going to make a ton of money for all of them.

DOWNSTAIRS, Alex and Max were popping tabs on cans again, but this time the cans were full of Coke.

"You overreacted," Alex told Max. "We weren't alcoholics."

"Yeah, right, sure," Max said. "We just drank too much every night and passed out and had hangovers."

Alex started to laugh in spite of himself and his misery. "We never passed out. You're exaggerating."

"But I was right, just the same," Max said.

"You were right." Alex leaned his head back and tried to take stock, equally miserable and relieved after the day he'd spent cleaning up the mess he'd made of his life. "What happened there? How did I lose my grip so fast?"

"You got Nina and didn't want to lose her and you panicked," Max said. "And she didn't help things any, telling you she wouldn't marry you so you'd be free to leave when you grew up. That's no way to treat a guy."

Alex scowled at him. "Don't pick on Nina."

Max shook his head. "Not me. I'm crazy about her."

Alex sat up. "Hey."

Max waved him back. "And she's crazy about you. She just has some stuff to work out."

"Well, how long is it going to take her?" Alex asked. "I want her back now, but she was gone all day, and she's not answering her phone. She even locked her window." He winced as he said it. That had been the unkindest cut of all.

"Well, it would help if you canceled the house contract and told Dad you weren't going to grow up to be a cardiologist," Max told him, exasperated. "You're not exactly innocent here."

Alex nodded. "I know. It's done. All of it. I told Dad today. I also told him that you were right, and I gave him AA's phone number. It won't do any good, but at least he's disgusted with both of us."

"Well, then," Max said. "You did all the right things. Go make your move."

Alex closed his eyes. "She called me a jerk less than twenty-four hours ago and locked her window. I think it might be a little soon to make my move."

Max looked at him with blatant pity. "And then there are those duck shorts you're wearing."

"Hey." Alex glared at him. "Don't make fun of these duck shorts. They remind me of Nina." He grew philosophical. "These are my lucky shorts. I get her when I wear these shorts."

Max closed his eyes and shook his head. "Now I remember why I drank when I was with you. When I'm sober, you sound like a moron. Let me get this straight. You're wearing your lucky duck shorts because you think that will get Nina back?"

"No," Alex said. "I'll get Nina back, anyway. But it's too soon to make my move. So I'm wearing the shorts because I miss her like hell, and they remind me of her."

"And when will you be making this move?" Max asked pointedly.

"When I get my nerve up," Alex said. "A hell of a time you picked for us to go teetotal."

CHARITY AND JESSICA LEFT at eleven, still discussing what a well-run book tour would entail, and Nina was left alone in her apartment with Fred.

Just what she wanted. Just what she'd told Alex she wanted.

Well, she'd lied. She wanted Alex. Not in that damn house, but she could talk him out of that. He didn't want that, either. He wanted the apartments and Fred and old movies and jogging and the ER. All she had to do was convince him that she wanted that, too, and that she believed in him. She hadn't had unconditional love before, she'd had a marriage where appearances were everything and being at the right party meant more than being with the right person. But with Alex, she'd had the right person. The problem was, she'd been living her life backward instead of understanding it backward.

It was time to go forward.

Fred wiped his nose on her leg.

"Alex loves me unconditionally, Fred," she told him. "I know that. There is no doubt in my mind. It's just my ego in the way. I wanted to give him a perfect body, and all he wanted was mine."

Fred whined.

"One Oreo," she said, and stood up to get him one, but then stopped, struck by an idea. "No, wait. I have some-

thing for you that's better than an Oreo," she said, and headed for the bedroom with him trotting after her.

Nina went to her drawer and pulled out the Incredibra, designed to make not-so-perfect women look like impossibly perfect centerfolds. Never again. "Here, Fred," she said, and dropped it in front of him. "It's all yours, buddy. Wear it with my blessing."

Fred grabbed the bra, looking as close to ecstasy as she'd ever seen him, and ran with it.

Nina stripped off her clothes and went to the mirror and stared at herself with the bedroom light on.

There was nothing wrong with her body. All right, it was softer than it had been, and her waist was thicker than it had been, and nothing about it could be called perky, but it was a good healthy body, and Alex loved it. *Playboy* would never come calling, but she didn't want *Playboy,* she wanted Alex.

Nina put on her trench coat, unlocked her living-room window and climbed down the fire escape to get him.

Of course, Max was there when she climbed in Alex's window. They were sitting across from each other, their feet on Alex's coffee table, drinking Coke, when they looked up and saw her.

Alex stood up first, but Max was only a beat behind. "I was just going," he told her. "And I've got to tell you, I've never left for a better reason."

Nina smiled at him and he grinned back.

"Leave, Max," Alex said, and Max said, "I'm already gone."

Then he was, and she was alone with Alex, not sure what to say or do next.

"I've missed you," Alex said, "and I was stupid."

"I've missed you, too," Nina said.

Then Alex set his jaw. "But if you've come here to tell me I'm too young for you to marry, you can crawl right back through that damn window. I mean it. I want it all this time."

Nina took a deep breath. The she untied her belt and dropped her trench coat and stood there naked in front of him, with all the living-room lights on.

"Oh, God." Alex walked toward her. "Forget the window. You stay away from that window. In fact, I'm having that window nailed shut, so you can forget about ever leaving me again."

She moved then, too, meeting him halfway across the room, closing her eyes as her naked body touched him, arching herself into him as he held her close and his hands moved down her back.

"God, I've missed you," he whispered into her hair. "I was going crazy trying to figure out how to get you back. What the hell were you doing all day and night?"

"I had Charity and Jessica up there." She leaned her head against his chest, so glad to be with him again and to have his hands on her again that she couldn't talk for a minute. "We were working things out. And when we worked those things out, I'd worked this out, too." She looked up at him. "I thought I'd never find anybody who'd love me enough that it wouldn't matter that I wasn't twenty again, so I decided I'd make sure I never needed anyone. And I did. I'm independent now and I can get by without anyone. Anyone but you."

Alex closed his eyes for a moment, and said, "Don't walk out on me again. Please. If I screw up, just tell me, but don't leave."

She shook her head. "Never. I couldn't ever leave you again."

He kissed her, softly at first so that she shuddered under his hands, but then harder, probing her mouth with his tongue, and she wanted him naked, lusted for the feel of his skin on hers, and she ran her hands under his T-shirt, sliding it up his body as she slid her palms up his chest. He sucked in his breath and then helped her pull the shirt over his head, moaning with her as her breasts touched his skin. His hands moved down to cup her breasts, his thumbs rough on her nipples and she pressed against him, craving the ache of his hands hard on her.

"Anything else you need to say?" he whispered in her ear. "Say it fast because in about another thirty seconds, I'm going to drag you to the floor, and then we're not talking anymore."

"Tell me you're not going to be a cardiologist and we don't have to live in that damn house." Nina let her hands slide down his back, smoothing her palms over the muscles there that clenched as she touched them. "I'll love you and stay with you anyway, no matter what, but you'll hate being a cardiologist, and I'll hate the house, and I don't care about the money."

"I'm not going to be a cardiologist." Alex bent his head until his forehead was against hers. "My father isn't speaking to me anymore, but the house is gone and I'm staying in the ER. Even Max is taking a two-month leave of absence. We're turning into human beings. At least I am. It's what I want."

Nina let her hands slip over his rear end, feeling the cotton of his shorts, rough against her palms after the smoothness of his skin. "It's what I want, too," she said, and then she hooked her thumbs in his waistband, and pulled his duck shorts down as she kissed her way down his stomach until she could take him in her mouth.

"You can have anything you want," Alex said, and his voice cracked. "Except separate beds. Oh, God, don't stop doing that."

Nina raked her nails down his thighs and sucked harder, and he moaned and moved against her while she lost herself in the sheer power of having him in her mouth, knowing she was making him mindless, loving the way he felt against her tongue. Then he pulled her away and fell to his knees, kissing her so hard her mouth throbbed before he pushed her on her back and bent his head to her. He bit at her hip before he licked inside her and made the lovely low heat she'd felt while she'd loved him explode into sudden, driving ache. "Don't stop," she breathed while he licked and sucked and made her blood bubble and her veins itch. "Don't ever, *ever* stop." She arched back as the need grew too hot, and then his hands moved under her hips, holding her tight against his mouth, while she writhed and screamed and came.

Then he was on his feet, yanking her to hers, pulling her dazed across the living room to his bedroom, stopping at the door to shove her against the wall and kiss her savagely, pressing her against the wall with his body while she scraped her nails down his sides and bit his lip. "Take me hard," she whispered to him and then he dragged her into the bedroom and fell with her on the bed, fumbling for the condom in his drawer while she slid against him, biting kisses down his side, until he pinned her under him and took her, driving into her over and over again mindlessly, until there was nothing in the world but the rhythm of their bodies, and the pulse of their blood and their gasps were the same as they rocked together into orgasm, shuddering and then finally quiet in each other's arms.

Hours later, Nina woke and moved her cheek against Alex's chest, listening to the beat of his heart, grateful it was such a strong one since they were obviously going to be risking cardiac arrest for the rest of their lives every time they made love. She felt him stir beneath her, felt his hand on her hair, and then she smiled as his hand moved down her shoulder and the slope of her back and patted her rear end.

"Hello," she said softly.

His hand moved to her waist and gathered her closer. "Hello," he said. "I like you naked. Never wear clothes again."

She smiled against his skin, too drunk with contentment to talk.

"Thanks for not bringing the Incredibra," he said, and she moved so she could see him.

He was looking at her with so much love that she closed her eyes for a minute, overwhelmed that he cared so much. "You're welcome," she whispered. "I love you."

"I love you, too," he whispered back and kissed her, moving his lips against hers so gently that she felt her body ache in response. Then he whispered against her cheek, "Do me a favor and throw that damn thing out. You're so beautiful without it."

"I gave it to Fred," she told him, and watched him smile, loving his smile, loving him. "It's his favorite thing to steal next to Oreos so I just gave it to him for keeps. He was thrilled."

"Good." Alex shifted against her, making all her nerve endings jump and throb, and evidently his, too, because he drew in a sharp breath. "He can wear it in the wedding." He grew still then, watching her, obviously waiting for her

to say that she couldn't marry him, that it was out of the question, that he was too young, that people would talk.

"Fred's going to be in our wedding?" she said, and he relaxed against her and laughed, and she held him close, completely sure of him and his love. Then he rolled to pin her under him and drive her out of her mind again.

"I see Fred as ring bearer," Alex said in her ear.

And six weeks later, so did everybody else.

Silhouette

SPECIAL EDITION™

SPECIAL EDITION

Stories of love and life, these powerful
novels are tales that you can identify with—
romances with "something special" added in!

Fall in love with the stories of authors such
as **Nora Roberts, Diana Palmer, Ginna Gray**
and many more of your special favorites—as
well as wonderful new voices!

Special Edition brings you
entertainment for the heart!

SSE-GEN

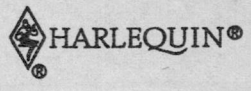 **HARLEQUIN®**

Not The Same Old Story!

HARLEQUIN PRESENTS® Exciting, emotionally intense romance stories that take readers around the world.

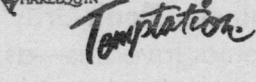 *Harlequin Romance®* Vibrant stories of captivating women and irresistible men experiencing the magic of falling in love!

HARLEQUIN® *Temptation* Bold and adventurous— Temptation is strong women, bad boys, great sex!

HARLEQUIN SUPERROMANCE® Provocative, passionate, contemporary stories that celebrate life and love.

 AMERICAN ROMANCE® Romantic adventure where anything is possible and where dreams come true.

HARLEQUIN® INTRIGUE® Heart-stopping, suspenseful adventures that combine the best of romance and mystery.

LOVE & LAUGHTER™ Entertaining and fun, humorous and romantic—stories that capture the lighter side of love.

HARLEQUIN SUPERROMANCE®

...there's more to the story!

Superromance. A *big* satisfying read about unforgettable characters. Each month we offer *four* very different stories that range from family drama to adventure and mystery, from highly emotional stories to romantic comedies—and much more! Stories about people you'll believe in and care about. Stories too compelling to put down....

Our authors are among today's *best* romance writers. You'll find familiar names and talented newcomers. Many of them are award winners—and you'll see why!

If you want the biggest and best in romance fiction, you'll get it from Superromance! Available wherever Harlequin books are sold.

LOOK FOR OUR FOUR FABULOUS MEN!

Each month some of today's bestselling authors bring four new fabulous men to Harlequin American Romance. Whether they're rebel ranchers, millionaire power brokers or sexy single dads, they're all gallant princes—and they're all ready to sweep you into lighthearted fantasies and contemporary fairy tales where anything is possible and where all your dreams come true!

You don't even have to make a wish...Harlequin American Romance will grant your every desire!

Look for Harlequin American Romance wherever Harlequin books are sold!

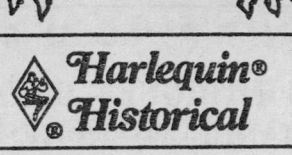

Harlequin® Historical

If you're a serious fan of historical romance,
then you're in luck!

Harlequin Historicals brings you
stories by bestselling authors, rising new stars
and talented first-timers.

Ruth Langan & Theresa Michaels
Mary McBride & Cheryl St.John
Margaret Moore & Merline Lovelace
Julie Tetel & Nina Beaumont
Susan Amarillas & Ana Seymour
Deborah Simmons & Linda Castle
Cassandra Austin & Emily French
Miranda Jarrett & Suzanne Barclay
DeLoras Scott & Laurie Grant...

You'll never run out of favorites.

Harlequin Historicals...they're too good to miss!

HARLEQUIN  PRESENTS®

HARLEQUIN PRESENTS
men you won't be able to resist falling in love with...

HARLEQUIN PRESENTS
women who have feelings just like your own...

HARLEQUIN PRESENTS
powerful passion in exotic international settings...

HARLEQUIN PRESENTS
intense, dramatic stories that will keep you turning
to the very last page...

HARLEQUIN PRESENTS
The world's bestselling romance series!

Harlequin Romance ®

Delightful
Affectionate
Romantic
Emotional
Tender
Original
Daring
Riveting
Enchanting
Adventurous
Moving

Harlequin Romance—the
series that has it all!

HROM-G